W9-BIG-438

Text Copyright © 1997 by Kevin Major
Wood Carvings Copyright © 1997 by Imelda George

All rights reserved. No part of this publication may be reproduced, stored in a retrieval system or transmitted in any form by any means electronic, mechanical, photocopying or otherwise without first obtaining written permission of the copyright owner.

Originally published in Canada by Red Deer College Press

This edition published in 1998 by SMITHMARK Publishers,
a division of U.S. Media Holdings, Inc.,
115 West 18th Street, New York, NY 10011.

SMITHMARK books are available for bulk purchase for sales promotion and premium use. For details write or call the manager of special sales, SMITHMARK Publishers, 115 West 18th Street, New York, NY 10011.

library of Congress Cataloging-In-Publication Data
Major, Kevin.
The story of the house of wooden Santas / story by Kevin Major; wood carvings by Imelda George; photography by Ned Pratt. -- 1st Smithmark ed.
p. cm.
Summary: Jesse's unemployed mother tries to make a new start for them by moving to a rural home where she hopes to foster a business carving figures for the Christmas season.
ISBN 0-7651-0829-1 (alk. paper)
[1. Santa Claus—Fiction. 2. Christmas—Fiction. 3. Mothers and sons—Fiction. 4. Moving, Household—Fiction.] I. George, Imelda, ill. II. Pratt, Ned, 1964- ill. III. Title.
PZ7.M2814Hr 1998
[Fic]--dc21 98-16810
CIP
AC

Printed in Hong Kong

10 9 8 7 6 5 4 3 2 1

THE STORY OF THE HOUSE OF WOODEN SANTAS

KEVIN MAJOR

WOOD CARVINGS BY IMELDA GEORGE

For Duncan

There was just Jesse and his mother.

But Jesse's mother had lost her job. She searched for months without finding another, and so she decided they should move out of the city to some place where it wasn't so expensive to live.

"No way," Jesse had said to her.

But her mind was made up. She sold off a pile of furniture and toys, and all the hockey equipment Jesse had outgrown. She packed up the old car and drove three hours on the highway, and down a side road another hour, until they reached the house she had read about in the ad.

The landlady, Mrs. Wentzell, met them at the front gate. She was a silver-haired woman with earrings that dangled like crazy, and a terrier in her arms that never stopped yapping.

"It's my daughter's house really," Mrs. Wentzell said. "They had to move away."

Jesse's mother was looking at the ocean beyond the house. "So beautiful," she sighed.

Jesse grunted. "Yeah. Right. Big deal."

Mrs. Wentzell's eyes narrowed in on Jesse. "My granddaughter is about your age. She loved it here."

When Mrs. Wentzell wasn't looking, Jesse sneered at the dog. The dog bared its pointed little teeth and growled.

"Ivan!"

Mrs. Wentzell clamped the jaws of the dog shut with her hand.

"Ivan the Terrier," muttered Jesse to himself. "Mighta known."

"I'm starting a business," his mother explained to Mrs. Wentzell. "Years ago I took up wood carving as a hobby . . . making figures, angels mostly. Now I've decided to try it full time. I've made a deal with a craft shop to carry my carvings." She paused. "I'll have the rent money to you as soon as they start to sell."

Mrs. Wentzell hesitated. "I don't know what my husband would have said. . . . "

"It'll work out. I'm sure of it."

Mrs. Wentzell finally nodded.

Jesse's mother started down the lane toward the house, a smile lighting her face.

Jesse followed glumly behind, down the lane to the front door.

TWENTY-FOUR DAYS TO CHRISTMAS

This Friday, the first day of December, Jesse burst through the same front door, home from school. He headed straight for the television, plunked himself down in front of it, set to play video games and watch cartoons.

His mother came marching out from the workroom, where she had been all day. A tough look of determination was set into her face.

She flicked off the TV and stood in front of it, her arms folded like an iron guard from one of the games he was about to play. "It's wonderful outside," his mother declared. "The fresh air will do you good."

Jesse erupted with a chorus of complaints. "It's boring here. They don't even have a hockey league. There's no shopping mall. There's not even a place to buy a hamburger!"

"Surely there are other things you could do," his mother insisted. "Christmas is coming. Santa is on his way. You *could* be getting ready for him."

"He probably won't even find this place . . . if there is a Santa, which I doubt!"

"Oh, Jesse."

Jesse pressed his lips together and stalked off.

He left his mother standing there, her arms still folded. She walked slowly back to her workroom.

Jesse banged his bedroom door shut.

Late that night, when his eyes were too heavy to open, he heard his mother creep into his room. She placed something on his bedside table and whispered close to his ear.

"In the House of Wooden Santas there's someone to keep you safe and take away your doubts. *Guardian Santa* protects you from the worries of the world." She planted a kiss on his cheek.

During the night Jesse stirred in his bed. Noise from another part of the house touched his sleep. His eyes drifted open for a few moments, just long enough for a vision of Santa Claus to fly into his dreams.

MASON

TWENTY-THREE DAYS TO CHRISTMAS

Jesse woke with a start, his head filled with Santa hovering in the air above him.

He blinked. He sat up quickly in bed. He looked up and down and around his room, and especially long at his bedside table. His room was just the same.

And he was sure his Saturday morning would be just the same. Bor-r-r-ring.

He fell back on the bed and thought of how he used to be up at seven, into his hockey gear, and at the apartment door, waiting for his mother to drive him to the arena. He could still hear the cheering crowd when he scored the winning goal in the second game of the play-offs. He looked over at the gold medal that hung off the corner of his dresser mirror.

Jesse crawled out of bed and made his way toward the living room, ready to curl up on the sofa in front of the TV. When he entered the room he came to a sudden stop. It was as if he had stepped into another world. He rubbed the sleep out of his eyes.

The room was filled with Christmas! Garlands of evergreens laced with silver stars and colored paper ribbon swirled up and over the windows and doors. On the walls hung wreaths wound red with dogberries, trimmed with dried flowers and herbs, cinnamon sticks and pine cones flecked with gold. Crepe paper chains streamed from the ceiling, heaps of nuts crowded the mantelpiece, and about it all drifted the smell of the woods and the crackling sound of fire in the fireplace.

The room had been cleared of all its furniture, except the old sofa and end tables. Not another thing remained. Including his video games. Including the TV.

"Mom!"

His mother emerged from her workroom, smelling still of evergreens, wood chips clinging to the wool of her sweater. In her hands she held a box. She laid it between them on the sofa.

Jesse looked at her, a squirming look, full of questions.

"Well," she said, "what do you think?"

"You did all this? Last night? After I went to bed?"

"I'm determined this is going to be our best Christmas ever."

She set the lid of the box aside. Pushing back the crumpled newspaper, she smiled as if to greet a friend.

"Something new I've been working on."

From the box she lifted a wooden figure, turning it upright so Jesse could see. She placed it in his hands. His fingers ran over the painted wood for a moment, and then he looked at his mother. A bit of a smile slumped across his face. He laid the figure on the mantel above the fireplace.

When he sat back on the sofa, his mother said, "Into the House of Wooden Santas comes a fine old chap. Some call him St. Nick or Father Christmas or Kris Kringle. I call this guy *Santa from Long Ago.* 'Cause he's come through snow and rain, across vast deserts, and over the seven seas. . . . "

"Mom . . . " Jesse groaned.

His mother looked at him. Her eyebrows narrowed.

"I'm getting too old for this stuff! I'm nine," he protested.

"Nobody's too old for a little magic in their lives! Look at me."

Jesse rolled his eyes. There was a long silence. He folded his arms and sat staring at the fire. His mother stared at the fire, too, and hummed "Santa Claus is Coming to Town" and pretended not to care.

"I like that figure," Jesse said finally. "I thought you only carved angels."

"I'm branching out."

"Oh."

"I'm expanding."

"Good."

There was another long silence.

"Okay. So can I keep him?"

His mother didn't say anything.

"Can I?"

"For today," she said. "We need the money."

"Knew it."

"There'll be others . . . in other outfits."

"Yeah, right."

"There will. I promise. I've been as busy as an elf in that workroom."

He sank into the sofa. "Now can I watch TV?"

His mother sat stiffly. Finally she gave in, went to another room, and lugged the TV back.

From time to time that day, during the commercials mostly, Jesse glanced at the mantel to check out Santa. The old guy seemed to gaze straight off into the distance, not paying him any attention.

"You for real?" Jesse muttered to himself at the end of the day, when his TV watching was over and it was time for bed. He was curled up on the sofa, in his pajamas, his bare feet stuck between the cushions.

His mother brought in a mug of hot chocolate for each of them. She turned off all the lights and they sat together in the glow of the fire. It seemed to make the room quietly shimmer.

"We should do this every night," chirped his mother, sipping her hot chocolate. "We could sit and chat. You could tell me about your day and I could tell you about mine."

"Bor-r-r-ring."

"No way," replied his mother as she looked up at the mantel. "Right, Santa? Not with Christmas coming. No way."

TWENTY-TWO DAYS TO CHRISTMAS

When Jesse's eyes were closed the Santa did seem real. Or was it a dream? Did he see the light flicker in the fellow's lantern?

The next morning he ran from the bedroom only to find his mom sound asleep on the sofa. She had a book on her stomach with her finger between the pages. She was in the same clothes she had been wearing the night before.

His eyes jumped to the mantel. Santa with the lantern was gone. But in his place was another guy. It looked to be Santa nestled in an armchair. Jesse stepped closer and discovered an open book in his lap.

Jesse looked at his mother and banged his foot against the brass guard in front of the fireplace. Her breathing fluttered. He banged it harder and she woke.

"Gosh," she said, "I don't even remember closing my eyes." She sat up. "I told you he'd be back. The House of Wooden Santas has a fellow who sure loves books — good ol' *Reading Santa.* I'd say this guy hardly turns on a television."

Jesse's head swerved to another part of the room. To where the TV was *supposed* to be. "Again!" he yelled.

"And this time it's not coming back."

"Mom!"

"I've thought it over very carefully and I've decided it's best for both of us. Maybe now you'll see there are other things you could be doing."

"No TV! Not even one program?"

"Not one."

Jesse moaned. "Sick."

"And that means video games, too."

"Really sick."

"It'll be fun. You'll find lots to do."

Jesse sat rigidly on the sofa. He tried to imagine his world without television. What would he do while he was waiting for supper? What would he do on Saturday mornings? What would he do in the middle of a snowstorm?

"Bor-r-r-ring," he told his mother. "Extremely and absolutely bor-r-r-ring."

"Santa doesn't think so."

Jesse turned his eyes to the mantel. The fellow did look happy. But only because his mother had made him that way. And besides, he didn't get dragged away to live in some place where there was never anything to do!

"I bet you can't do it," his mother said.

Jesse knew what his mother was up to and wasn't about to fall into her trap. He sat on the sofa

Twas the Night
before Christmas
And all through
house

and hardly moved. He pretended not to hear a thing she was saying. The longer she talked the more he stiffened, until she gave up and went to the kitchen to make pancakes.

At the breakfast table, just as he was pouring on the syrup, his mother said, "This is Sunday. So what do you say we go to church?"

Jesse didn't reply.

"Maybe we'll see someone we know. Maybe you'll see some of your friends from school."

Jesse sneered. "I don't have any."

Church did turn out to be better than Jesse expected. The pews were as hard as those in his old church, but the music was a lot better. There was even a guitar and drums, and sometimes people clapped their hands to the songs.

After the service Jesse's mother tugged him off to social hour in the church basement. He had just bitten into a chocolate cupcake when he realized Mrs. Wentzell was standing next to them.

"Good morning," their landlady said to his mother. She was looking grouchier, Jesse thought, than she did with the yappy dog in her arms.

"Good morning."

"And how's your business doing?"

"It's a bit early yet. But with Christmas and all, I expect it will pick up, Mrs. Wentzell. Any day now."

"I hope so. For your sake, and the boy's."

"I'm sure it will."

"You can't expect to raise a child without a steady income."

Mrs. Wentzell looked at Jesse, whose mouth was full of cupcake. It was so full, in fact, that crumbs were starting to spill down his chin. She handed him a napkin.

"Thank you," Jesse mumbled. That caused a spurt of more crumbs.

"Jobs are not easy to come by these days," his mother said to Mrs. Wentzell.

"I know that well enough. My daughter had to go all the way to Vancouver."

"That's a shame. And you won't get to see your granddaughter this Christmas?"

Mrs. Wentzell just frowned and left. She hadn't even finished her tea, Jesse noticed. She went out the door, past the minister, who had just walked into the room.

The minister joined Jesse and his mother.

She held out her hand. "Michelle Agnew," she said to his mother. She smiled broadly at Jesse. "I'm the leader of this flock."

Jesse gave her a strange look.

"I'm no sheep," he said.

"And nobody can pull the wool over your eyes, right?"

The two women laughed. Jesse forced a smile.

TWENTY-ONE DAYS TO CHRISTMAS

On school days Jesse had been used to his breakfast on his lap and a half-hour of cartoons. Today his mother insisted he join her in the kitchen. He dragged himself to the table.

"Go-o-o-od morning, my treasure. And what would you like on your cereal this fine and sunny morning?"

She held a banana above his bowl, with a small knife ready to slice it into pieces. She was even singing. "Here comes Santa Claus, here comes Santa Claus, right down Santa Claus Lane. . . . "

"Whatever," Jesse mumbled.

Down came the banana slices. "Sugar?"

"Whatever."

"Under the tea cosy."

Not exactly where he would have thought to look, but his mother had done stranger things before.

Jesse lifted the tea cosy. His hand jumped back in surprise. Not a sugar bowl, but another Santa.

"Oh, my," said his mother. "And what have we here?"

As if she didn't know, thought Jesse.

"Popping up in the House of Wooden Santas . . . is . . . *Santa the Woodworker.* He drives a fine nail and strokes a steady saw. And to us he comes complete, house and all!"

Not a word from Jesse.

"Think Santa could build us a house of our own?"

"Wish for it on Christmas Eve," Jesse shot back.

He looked at his mother. She was suddenly quiet. He could see a little sadness in her eyes.

"We're okay, Mom."

She winked his way and showed a bit of a smile. "I guess we've managed so far."

She put an arm around him.

"You're right," she said, her voice quiet. "And I was rather greedy. Santa is for the small stuff."

"Mom, you're squeezing me too hard."

She gave him a slobbery kiss.

"Oh, man." He wiped his cheek with the end of his T-shirt and ran off to get dressed for school. He was out the door then, and through the snow to the bus stop.

He wasn't looking forward to school, as boring as the weekend might have been. School meant work and sitting next to Jonathan.

Jonathan was a torment and he bragged a lot. Especially about his father. It drove Jesse crazy.

If anyone in class had a new game, Jonathan was sure to have played it already with his father. If anyone's dad had a new snowmobile, his father had a better one that went twice as fast. And he knew everything about hockey, Jonathan said, because he'd played it all his life. Plus he met Wayne Gretzky once in an airport.

When Jesse walked into the classroom he quietly asked his teacher if he could be moved, but Mr. O'Donnell whispered, "Hang in there. Jonathan is going through a little bit of a rough time." Mr. O'Donnell smiled at Jesse and left it at that. Jesse walked down the aisle.

Jonathan was already in his seat. Jesse checked his chair before sitting down. The last day it had been gum, and the day before that, melted snow.

"You're in big trouble," Jonathan said to him.

"Me?"

"You'll have to go to the office."

"Yeah, right."

"Yep."

"What for?"

"Marking on your desk."

Jesse looked down. In one corner of his desk, the corner closest to Jonathan, were three words, in rough, heavy pencil letters. They stood out like dirty scars.

They said: *DON'T BELIEVE IT.* Jesse quickly covered the words with his hand.

"You did that," he snapped at Jonathan.

"No way."

Jesse spit on his fingers and slipped them under the hand covering the words. He rubbed hard. He peeked under his hand and saw that most of it was smeared away. He wet his fingers again and rubbed away what was left. Just in time, too, for Mr. O'Donnell was standing at the front of the class, his eagle eyes looking directly at them.

As soon as Mr. O'Donnell turned away, Jonathan started bugging Jesse again. "So, you still believe in Santa Claus. My father says — "

"I don't care what your father says!"

"If you're afraid you won't get presents, that's dumb because you still do."

"You're what's dumb," Jesse said.

Mr. O'Donnell appeared at that moment and stood near their seats like a jackrabbit ready to jump. They stopped talking and started their work. Mr. O'Donnell eased back into his regular, swinging walk. Jesse wished more than ever that he could be moved.

When he arrived home from school that day he was feeling extra sour.

"Okay," his mother said, "what's the big deal? Out with it. I'm all ears."

But Jesse just went off to his room and pretended he had homework to do. When his mother came in and sat on the bed he still refused to talk about it.

"Okay. Suit yourself," she said. "Bet Santa understands."

She left the room. He heard her go into her workroom at the back of the house.

Jesse grunted. "Yeah, right."

TWENTY DAYS TO CHRISTMAS

On Tuesday morning Jesse could have stayed in bed forever. No way did he want to get up, even though he'd been tossing and turning for hours.

He lay on his back with the bedclothes tight under his chin, trying to figure out why Jonathan was being so mean. And he could not get out of his head the words Jonathan had scrawled on his desk.

Maybe Jonathan was right. Maybe his mother was playing a game with him. Maybe there was no such . . .

Suddenly something caught his eye. He sprang upright in bed. Suspended from the curtain rod, in the middle of his window, was Santa, tucked inside the curve of a golden crescent moon.

Jesse scrambled to his feet so he was eye to eye with the fellow. His mother, yawning and tying her housecoat, shuffled in at that moment. She stood at the foot of the bed. Now all three of them were at eye level, though his mother's eyes were not open all the way.

"In the House of Wooden Santas," she said sleepily, "hangs our *Santa in the Moon.*"

She held Santa to one side and let go, causing him to swing silently back and forth, back and forth, in front of the window. "He rides high in the sky," she said. She stopped for a few seconds because of a wide yawn. "Takes away the troubles of the day and gently rocks us through the night."

"Mighta worked for you," Jesse said and bounced to the floor. "Sure didn't work for me."

It spoiled his mother's daydream smile. "Jesse," she pleaded with a whine in her voice as he went through the door, "wait."

She stood in the hallway, leaning against the wall outside the bathroom door.

He emerged from the bathroom and glared at her. "Is there such a thing as privacy in this house?" He padded over the wooden floor, straight to the living room sofa. She was right behind him.

"Do you mind?" he said, frowning stiffly, his arms clasped around his legs.

"Jesse, what's the matter? You can tell your mother."

He jumped up and ran off back to his room. He hauled on his clothes. He was determined not to cry, even though he came close to it every time he thought about having to go to school.

Santa's swing back and forth in front of the window had almost stopped. When Jesse finished dressing, he fixed his eyes on him. But filling Jesse's head, like a fearsome drift of swirling snow, was Jonathan's silly grin and his mean and teasing words.

When Jesse arrived in school that morning he pretended he had no time to even look at Jonathan.

But before long, small folded scraps of paper landed on his desk. Jesse ignored them.

Then came the whispers. Jesse tried to ignore them, too. But words crept through, muffled words jabbing at him. "Wimpy . . . bet you believe in elves, too." Followed by a chuckle under Jonathan's breath.

Jesse wanted to look him in the face and roar at him to shut his mouth. But all Jesse did was lean his head against his hand to cover his ear.

There was only one bright spot in his life during the whole school day. Mr. O'Donnell decided on the parts for the Christmas concert.

"For the very important role of the first shepherd," he said, "how about you, Jesse?"

Jesse nodded. He was thrilled to be the first one picked.

"The shepherds are the narrators," said Mr. O'Donnell, "and I know I can count on you to speak clearly and look serious."

"Yes, sir."

Mr. O'Donnell's eyes scanned the room. "For the other shepherd . . . "

Hands shot up all around.

"This part is just as important. At times every single person in the audience will be looking at you . . . Jonathan."

"Yes!" shouted Jonathan.

Jesse's heart sank.

"Jesse, I'm counting on you to help Jonathan *stay* serious. We wouldn't want any grinning or giggling."

"No, sir," Jonathan sighed.

Mr. O'Donnell turned his attention to choosing the other parts.

Jonathan looked over at Jesse. A devilish grin spread slowly across his face.

NINETEEN DAYS TO CHRISTMAS

Jesse moaned. He groaned. He buried his head in his pillow.

And when his mother entered his room, as he knew she would, he sounded especially miserable.

"Poor baby," she sighed. "Let Mommy have a look."

He took that to be a good sign. Whenever he was sick his mother treated him like a four-year-old.

"My stomach."

She touched it and he flinched.

She frowned even more. "Poor tummy." She drew in a great breath. "Appendicitis."

"No!" he proclaimed. He forgot to moan as he was saying it, so he said it again, "No-o-o-o."

"How can you tell, sweetie?"

"I don't have a fever." He took her hand and put it to his forehead. "And it's not a sharp pain in my stomach. It's kinda like that time I ate too much chocolate."

"Do you feel like you want to throw up?"

Jesse hadn't thought of that. "Well, sort of."

He could see his mother was starting to have doubts, so he shut his eyes and let his head rest on the pillow, moaned slightly again, and pretended to be falling asleep.

She kissed him gently on the forehead. "Maybe you just need more rest. A day home from school."

Finally. The words he had been waiting for. But he didn't stir. He just moaned a sleepy "okay."

Only when he heard his mother leave the room and the door creak behind her did his eyes pop open. He breathed a sigh of relief.

Ah, a day without Jonathan pestering him. A day to himself. If only he had TV.

He heard the door creak. His eyes snapped shut.

He felt the edge of the bed sink under the weight of his mother. He felt the touch of her hand against his cheek.

She tucked something partway under the covers and against his chest. It felt hard. Then she placed his hand gently over it.

She whispered, "In the House of Wooden Santas, snuggled away, is *Snoozing Santa.* He wants you to get plenty of rest."

There was a long silence.

Jesse didn't dare move a muscle. But his brain was doing cartwheels. Oh boy, oh boy, he thought, she's really done it this time. She's turning Santa Claus into a teddy bear. She had her son cuddling into a piece of wood, for heaven's sake. He could end up with a splinter in his chest.

As soon as she was out the door, Jesse turned over on his back and examined the poor guy. He was sound asleep, and Jesse couldn't help but imagine his dreams.

Jesse laid the Santa on his bedside table, stared at him, and nestled down as comfortably as he was.

Jesse tried smiling.

He drifted off to sleep.

He was awakened by voices in the kitchen. At first they floated in and out of his head, bits of talk poking at his dreams. The voices seemed to grow louder and give way often to bursts of laughter.

Soon Jesse was wide awake, wondering who besides his mother could be in the kitchen.

He could tell it was a woman. He slipped out of bed and tiptoed to the door. He didn't dare open it wider because it would creak. The best he could do was shut one eye and peer through the crack with the other.

He caught sight of the two of them at the kitchen table, drinking tea. He could see part of the woman's face. It was the minister from the church they had been to on Sunday.

More laughter.

"I better go, I'm afraid." Their voices grew faint as they headed toward the front door. "Thanks for the tea."

"And we'll see you tomorrow afternoon."

"Jonathan's got a net in the basement. The boys can play hockey."

Jonathan? The shock of it caused Jesse to bang his head against the edge of the door. He stumbled back to bed. It couldn't be.

But before long Jesse found out that indeed it was the very same Jonathan.

"Reverend Agnew dropped by and I was mentioning how you were having a little trouble getting used to a new place," his mother said, "and, lo and behold, doesn't she have a boy in your class at school! Now isn't that a lucky coincidence? Just what the doctor ordered."

She was going on and on and hardly stopping for a breath. She took one of Jesse's hands and patted it as she continued full speed ahead.

"I know you're not feeling the best right now, but tomorrow you'll be back to your old self. And after school we'll go over to Jonathan's house, and you two can get to know each other even better than you do now. And won't that be loads of fun?"

"Yeah."

"You don't sound very excited."

"I'm sick, remember." Though he couldn't even manage a moan.

"Ah, poor baby. And here's your mommy keeping you awake."

Jesse's mother pecked his cheek with a kiss, and as she slipped out of the room she whispered, "Just let yourself dream of all the wonderful things your tomorrows will bring."

The door creaked shut.

Jesse moaned.

EIGHTEEN DAYS TO CHRISTMAS

In the early hours of the morning Jesse heard the wind howl. He could picture a wild storm, gusts of snow so fierce the school would never open.

After one especially loud howl Jesse sprang to the window, only to find there was not a flake of snow in the air. Disgusting. What was the use of stupid wind without any snow?

"Forecast calls for a perfect day," came his mother's voice above the sound of the radio in the kitchen.

"Some chance," Jesse muttered.

He strolled to the kitchen, knowing it was no use to look sick again. His mother would have him out the door and straight to the doctor's office.

"How's your tummy?" she asked.

"Better."

"Knew it." She patted his head. "Terrific."

Breakfast was cinnamon toast burnt around the edges and orange juice that had been mixed with too many cans of water.

"Sorry about that," she said. "I don't know where my mind is this morning."

"Outer space," Jesse said. And his mother didn't even notice.

All during breakfast Jesse expected a new Santa to pop up. His eyes wandered around the kitchen, but there was nothing. After breakfast he took the long way back to his bedroom, through the rest of the house. Nothing there either. He was tempted to peek in the workroom, but then his mother might think he actually looked forward to her Santas.

All the way to school his *own* mind was in outer space.

In his classroom he avoided looking at Jonathan for as long as possible. When he finally did glance his way it was because Jonathan had not uttered a word.

Jonathan's head hung down and his eyes were not budging from the math book in front of him. The book was open to the wrong page.

At recess and lunch hour Jonathan kept to himself and said he had other, more important things to do. When they practiced for the Christmas concert Jonathan knew every one of his lines and didn't laugh once.

Weird, very weird, Jesse said to himself.

When the bell rang at the end of the day, he and Jonathan went their separate ways. And still Jonathan had not said a word to him.

Jesse's mother picked him up and they were off to the grocery store. At the check-out counter she discovered she didn't have enough money with her, and had to put three cans back on the shelves.

Still in outer space, thought Jesse.

At four o'clock they pulled into the driveway of Jonathan's house. As they started up the path Jesse's stomach tightened.

Jonathan's mother met them at the back door. "Come on in. I just this minute put on the kettle."

Jonathan was sitting at the kitchen table, doing his homework and looking just as serious as he had in school.

"You boys can play hockey in the basement," his mother said.

Jonathan disappeared down the stairs as soon as the words were out of her mouth.

Jesse looked at his mother. He could see he was expected to go, too.

He headed to the stairs and almost ran into a man with a walking stick.

"Sorry," Jesse stammered.

"It's okay."

The man wasn't pleased, Jesse could tell, even though there was something like a smile on his face.

"This is Jonathan's dad."

"Oh," Jesse said. He didn't mean to sound surprised. He was thinking, Is this who Jonathan is always bragging about?

He limped past Jesse. He sure didn't look in any shape to drive a snowmobile. Or play hockey.

Partway down the stairs Jesse heard his mother's voice in the kitchen. "Glad to meet you. Michelle tells me you're interested in wood carving."

Jesse stopped to listen.

"I could be, I guess. There's not much to do when you're sick of watching television."

"I'd be happy to give you a few pointers."

"If you want. It's not my idea. But, of course, you know that."

Jesse continued down the steps. Jonathan handed him a hockey stick.

"Fell off a ladder a few months ago and busted his hip," Jonathan muttered. "Had to get a steel pin in it. He's pretty mad with himself for what happened."

"Is it getting better?"

"Not like it should."

The two of them played floor hockey. They took turns being goalie and taking shots on each other. Jonathan didn't brag, even when he scored on Jesse. And not once did he mention about not believing in anything.

His mother brought them fudge cookies and milk, and they sat on the bottom steps and talked hockey. Just like he remembered doing with his friends in the city.

When Jonathan asked him his favorite team in the NHL, he told him the Leafs and Jonathan went, "Yes!" under his breath. Then he said, "My dad said we might fly up and see an NHL game. But I guess maybe we won't now."

"My mom said we might. But I guess maybe we can't afford it."

When it was finally time for Jesse to leave, he asked his mom, "Just five minutes more?"

And as soon as Jesse got home that evening he kicked off his boots and ran to his bedroom to dig out his binder of hockey cards.

He ran right into a new Santa.

A Santa on skates, holding a hockey stick, on top of his bedroom dresser.

"Yes!"

"Into the House of Wooden Santas," his mother declared, "skates *Hockey Santa.* Weaving down the ice, across the red line, over the blue line, past the defense. He shoots . . . "

"He scores!"

"Whatta guy!" she said.

"And he's gonna win 'em the Stanley Cup." Jesse held Santa over his head like a trophy, pretending to skate around the room and shouting, "Yes!"

"Yes," agreed his mother. "Finally. Yes!"

SEVENTEEN DAYS TO CHRISTMAS

As soon as Jesse arrived in school on Friday morning he raced off to find Jonathan. He couldn't wait to show him his hockey card collection, especially his Leaf rookies.

Jonathan took one look and said, "So. Big deal. I got a lot better cards than that."

Jesse snapped his binder shut and walked away.

But not before Jonathan called out to him, "If you believe hard enough, maybe Santa Claus will bring you *Gretzky's* rookie card." It was followed by a dumb laugh.

That card cost hundreds of dollars and Jonathan knew it. It was a rotten thing to say.

Still, Jesse couldn't keep himself from turning around and yelling, "Maybe I will!"

At his desk Jesse thought back to the day before and their good time together. He couldn't believe it was the same fellow.

"They tell you something's true, and then it all turns out to be a pack of lies," Jonathan said. "My father told me so."

Jesse did his best to ignore him the whole day, even at the practice for the Christmas concert when they were standing shoulder to shoulder.

"Hey, guys, you're not very friendly shepherds," Mr. O'Donnell complained. At the end of the practice he asked about their costumes.

"Our moms are working on them," Jonathan said. "His mom is making him a staff. Maybe my dad is gonna make one for me."

Jesse just nodded.

After school, when he arrived home, his mother called from the kitchen, "I just this minute put a Christmas cake in the oven. Wanna lick the bowl?"

Jesse threw down his backpack and threw himself on the sofa. When his mother came into the living room he grunted and raised his lip in a sneer.

"Now what?" she said.

"Jonathan. I hate him," Jesse blurted out. "The guy bugs me and he's a rotten friend."

"What . . . ?"

"He's a pain. He doesn't care about anyone except himself. He's dumb and I never want to talk to him again!"

"Whoa," said his mother. She sat down next to him.

Jesse wiped his eyes and his nose, both at the same time, with the sleeve of his sweatshirt.

"Jonathan's dad is having a pretty tough time of it," his mother said. "The doctors told him he'd be walking on his own by now."

"So. I don't even have a father," Jesse snapped, "and I don't go around saying rotten stuff to people when they're supposed to be your friend."

"You have a father. . . . "

It was the first time Jesse had mentioned his father in a long time. He lived thousands of miles away, and they hadn't been together since Jesse was a baby. Since then it was only Jesse and his mom, except that his father would phone on his birthday and Christmas. There were times he wished he had a father to do things with — like go to hockey games and stuff — but he had his mother and she loved him so much sometimes that she squeezed him to bits. Like right at this very moment.

His mother finally let him go. "It's different. When you're used to having a father in the same house, I mean," his mother said quietly. "Jonathan's dad has a lot on his mind. He was a carpenter, and now he can't work."

Jesse wasn't satisfied.

"Maybe Jonathan gets upset."

"And gets mean with me. For no reason!"

Jesse was mixed up. He wanted to be mad at someone.

"And there's no Santa Claus!" he yelled.

"He said that?"

Jesse grunted, "Yes."

"And you believe him?"

Jesse didn't know what to believe. He was mad and confused and frustrated.

His mother slipped away to her workroom. She returned with a wooden figure in her hands. This Santa was tall and straight, and he carried a walking staff with a star on the top.

"In the House of Wooden Santas . . . "

"Mom," Jesse whined, "I'm sick of these Santa — "

She put a forefinger to his lips and continued, " . . . there's a lot of trust. Santa knows it's not easy to find, especially when people do mean and rotten things."

"So?" he snapped.

"To believe in Santa, you have to search it out, and when you find it, hold onto it with all your heart."

Grumbling silence.

"Trusty Santa we'll call him," she said. "How about that?"

Jesse folded his arms rigidly.

His mother placed Santa carefully on the mantel. "Now," she said, "I need to finish off your staff for the concert. I'm almost done."

Jesse wouldn't look at her. He wouldn't move a muscle.

Only after she had gone did his stiffness gradually slip away.

He glanced at Santa. Maybe it was the scent of pine branches lingering about the room, or the

smell of Christmas cake wafting in from the kitchen, but his mind seemed to drift away to some place where he and Santa Claus were walking down a road, each with a staff in hand.

The telephone rang. Jesse shook his head and blinked.

He dragged himself to the phone. "Hello."

"Sorry, okay?"

"What?"

"Sorry for being so mean in school, okay?"

It was Jonathan. Jesse couldn't think of what to say.

"You still there?"

"Sorry about your father," Jesse said weakly.

"This morning he was acting weird again. He's okay now."

"You gotta have trust," Jesse murmured. It slipped out. He hardly realized he had said it.

"Guess what?"

"What?"

"My dad made my staff today," Jonathan said, "and it's amazing."

"Yeah?"

"Got a star on top and everything. He said he got the idea from your mother. You gotta come over tomorrow and see it."

When Jesse hung up the phone his mother emerged from her workroom. "One shepherd's staff, especially for you. See what I put on the top of it."

"A star," said Jesse, before he even looked.

"Just like Santa's," his mother said.

"And Jonathan's," Jesse murmured, as he held it for the first time.

SIXTEEN DAYS TO CHRISTMAS

Saturday morning had been cartoon morning. But this Saturday Jesse found himself sitting on the sofa, shepherd's staff in his hand, looking at Santa and *his* staff on the mantel, and thinking about the Christmas concert.

It gave him the most curious feeling. As if he really was out in a grassy field at night. Among the noise and smell of hundreds of sheep. Under the brightness of a star.

When Jesse and his mother arrived at Jonathan's later that morning, Jonathan came rushing down the stairs to meet him, staff in hand.

He handed it to Jesse. It seemed another way of saying he was sorry.

"Jonathan couldn't get to sleep last night," his mother said. "So I told him to count sheep." She laughed.

In the living room they encountered Mr. Agnew. "Great job," Jesse's mother told him.

"Doesn't take much to carve a star."

"Takes a lot to follow one," Reverend Agnew piped up. "Sorry. Couldn't resist." She laughed again.

"We brought something to show you," said Jesse. "Wait till you see this guy."

His mother uncovered Santa from the box.

"Cool," Jonathan said. "And look at what he's got in his hand. Wicked."

Jonathan's mother was bursting with compliments. Jesse felt proud.

His mom put Santa into Mr. Agnew's hands. "You should give it a try."

He looked at the carving, and ran his fingers over the wood. He handed it back to her. "I don't think so."

"You could do it, Dad."

"Sure you could," Jesse's mother insisted. "It doesn't have to be a Santa. It could be anything. I started off with angels."

"Angels are simple," Jesse declared. "Even *I* could do an angel."

"Men don't do angels," Jonathan announced.

His mother bristled. "What did you say?"

"He could do ministers," Jonathan stammered.

"Or moose," Jesse added. "Christmas moose."

They all laughed, even Jonathan's father, a little.

Reverend Agnew led the boys out of the room. "We'll leave them to figure it out. I think you two should go outdoors and play. It's too nice a day to be inside. The fresh air will do you good."

Mothers are all the same, thought Jesse — excited by fresh air.

"Wanna build a rink in the backyard?" Jonathan asked.

His mother whispered, "His dad used to make one every year."

Jesse was none too keen on the idea, though he had to go. No outdoor rink could ever be as good as a real indoor one.

First they cleared away enough snow to form a rectangle, piling it up the sides, and flattening what was left to make it level. Jonathan called it big enough for a good game of hockey.

"Doubt it," Jesse muttered to himself.

According to Jonathan they had to stamp down what snow was left as hard as they could, then flood it. Flood it very carefully several times. It might be days before they would be able to skate on it.

Yeah, Jesse was thinking, skate on it, sure.

Once they saw his mother and Jonathan's father looking at them through a window. Jonathan smiled up at his dad and worked all the harder.

After the snow had been trampled down, Jonathan and his mother rigged up a hose from the laundry room in the basement.

Spraying the water was the only real fun of it, as far as Jesse could see. Jonathan acted like the expert, but he did give Jesse several turns. When they had finished the first flooding, Jonathan stood back and admired their handiwork.

"It's going to be a wicked rink," Jonathan proclaimed.

"Believe it when I see it," Jesse mumbled to himself.

They trailed inside, red-cheeked and starving, and shed their winter gear. Jonathan's mother took a sizzling dish of macaroni and cheese from the oven. The aroma sent the boys scrambling for chairs at the kitchen table.

Jesse's mother could hardly hold in her delight. Jesse could tell what she was thinking — that he had finally found a friend. That it might be the end of him complaining about having to move.

Before he left for home Jesse noticed Jonathan standing next to his father, eyeing the piece of wood in his lap. His dad still wasn't looking too happy, but he was being nicer to Jonathan, acting a bit more like Jesse imagined a father would.

All the way back home in the car, Jesse thought about his own dad. He wondered what his dad would say to him if they met. He wondered if he would know where to phone him this Christmas.

His mother stopped to put Santa in the mail, and back at their house she went straight to her workroom.

That evening she set a small table in front of the window that looked out into the backyard. It was a still, crisp night and the naked porch light caught snowflakes drifting silently from the sky. The fresh glaze of snow sparkled as if it were diamond dust that had fallen over the ground.

Jesse's mom covered the table with a cloth and laid out two china plates and two crystal wine glasses that once belonged to her grandmother. In the center of the table she placed a lit candle, and next to it the newest Santa.

She called to Jesse in her best imitation of a butler, "Dinner is served."

She escorted him to his seat and pointed out their special guest. "Santa, this is Jesse. Jesse, Santa."

"Very pleased to meet you," he said. "Nice shovel you have there."

His mother shook out a napkin with a great flourish and spread it across Jesse's lap. "Can I interest you in some wine, sir?"

"Yes, please."

"Orange or brown."

"Brown."

She poured root beer into their wine glasses.

Jesse lifted his to his nose and sniffed it. "Wonderful fizz."

She uncovered the food. "And for you, sir — chicken legs. Done just the way you like them."

"Ah, superb."

"With peas, fresh from the can."

"Exquisite."

"Shall we begin?"

"Why not?"

"But first we must toast our special guest."

They raised their glasses.

"To a robust man of the great outdoors," said his mother. "Welcome to the House of Wooden Santas. No matter how much snow, he always loves to shovel. He's our — "

"I got it, I got it," said Jesse. "He's our *Fresh Air Santa.*"

"How did you ever guess?"

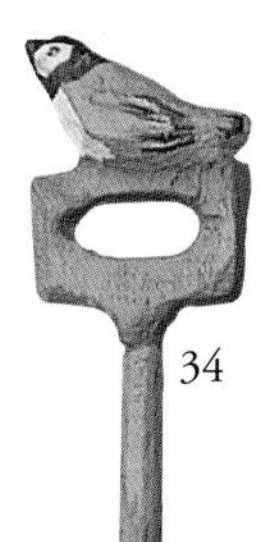

FIFTEEN DAYS TO CHRISTMAS

Jesse sat in the car, making silly faces, trying to pass the time until they reached the church.

The service was as lively as the week before, and Jesse found himself singing along with his mother and clapping his hands. He especially liked it when the drummer did the loud bit on the cymbals.

Partway through the service Jesse spied Jonathan sitting by himself several pews away. Jonathan did his spook face that he sometimes did in school when he was tired of listening to the teacher. Jesse flared his nostrils and puffed out his cheeks and made his goof eyes.

Someone in the pew behind tapped him on the shoulder. Jesse's head swiveled round instantly. His goof eyes looked right into the eyes of Mrs. Wentzell! Her head jumped back and her dangling earrings swung like crazy.

She leaned forward to Jesse's mother and said in a low, grumbling voice, "Your boy is being extremely rude."

Jesse turned to his mother and shrugged.

His mother looked back, confused. At the sight of the scowling landlady her eyes grew wide. She offered a half smile, but it did nothing to change the look on Mrs. Wentzell's face.

Jesse glanced at his mom. She was staring straight ahead. She glanced at Jesse. And rolled her eyes.

They sat stiffly together in the pew and stayed that way until, in the middle of the service, Reverend Agnew told a funny story and they both laughed out loud.

Jonathan's mother was good at telling stories, though Jesse could see that not everyone liked them. He sneaked a look behind. The landlady was looking even more grim.

Reverend Agnew paused for a few seconds. "I know some of you have been used to a more solemn service. In church we can be solemn, and in church we can also be joyful. Let's sing together, number three on your song sheet, 'I've got that joy, joy, joy, joy, down in my heart.'"

Just as the first notes were struck on the guitar, Jesse heard a muttering from Mrs. Wentzell. "Disgraceful. My husband would never have allowed the church to be turned into a dance hall." With that she took her prayer book and walked out of the church.

Later that afternoon Jesse heard about the reason for Mrs. Wentzell's sudden departure.

Jonathan and his mom had come by their house. With the school concert only a couple of days away, the mothers had set to work on the shepherds' costumes.

The boys were out of sight in Jesse's bedroom, playing with Lego. But the door was wide open and Jesse heard every word. It seemed Mrs. Wentzell could get pretty crabby when she set her mind to it.

"She sees things a certain way and she's not about to change. She's even worse since her husband died. She hasn't got much patience."

"I know," said Jesse's mom. "She's been calling me and calling me about the rent."

"Can you make a go of it with your carvings? It can't be easy."

"The craft store tells me it should pick up."

"You're sure?"

"I still have a few savings. We'll see."

Jesse walked into the kitchen. He stared at his mother to see how worried she looked.

"Okay, stand up on the chair," his mother said.

She sounded like her regular self.

"Let's see if we can make a shepherd out of you."

She had taken an old bathrobe and cut it down to fit him and used the leftover material for a headpiece. Jonathan's mom helped her tie rope around his head and his waist. When they had finished they looked very pleased with themselves.

His mother found his staff and put it in his hand.

"Never have I seen a more handsome shepherd."

"Doesn't look too ba-a-a-ad," Reverend Agnew said.

Jonathan emerged from the bedroom, anxious not to miss any of the fun. He stood on a chair next to Jesse. Soon there was a pair of handsome shepherds.

"Ewe two look great," Reverend Agnew declared. "Get it — *ewe."*

She was still chuckling when she and Jonathan went out the door, heading home.

Jesse's mother plopped down on the sofa. She looked exhausted. But before long she was up again and on her way to the workroom.

"Mom, you're working too hard. You need to take a break."

"I won't be much longer."

"Are we okay? Are we getting to be broke?"

His mother came to a sudden stop at her workroom door. She walked back to Jesse, sat down in a chair, and held both his hands.

"This is an experiment. Maybe it'll work out, maybe it won't. I have to admit, it hasn't been great so far. I guess it takes time for people to get to know my work. But I believe I can do it, and that should count for a lot."

She hugged him.

"What's this Santa?" Jesse said to cheer her up.

"So, you're looking forward to them now, are you?"

"Well, you know." He forced a grin. "I gotta be there when you need me."

She took his hand and led him to her workroom.

It was the one part of the house he stayed away from most of the time. He knew his mother didn't like it when he showed up unexpectedly and started poking around.

On a table was a Santa, nearly complete.

"Who is he?" Jesse noticed he didn't look particularly jolly.

"He has a lot on his mind, this guy. *Thinking Santa* maybe. What do you say, Jesse? He sits around the House of Wooden Santas thinking about how lucky he is to have people who care about him."

She turned the Santa and now Jesse could see into his eyes.

"And maybe," she said, "he's thinking how tough it is sometimes to have people who depend on him so much."

"He's thinking too hard if you ask me," Jesse declared. "People can only do the best they can do, Mom. That's what you always say."

"Think so?"

"Know so," he said.

He flared his nostrils and made his goof eyes — and kissed his mother on the cheek.

FOURTEEN DAYS TO CHRISTMAS

For once Jesse was looking forward to school. His mother bundled his costume into a bag, and with help from his shepherd's staff he trudged his way through the snow to the bus stop.

Jonathan met him as soon as he stepped off the bus. "We got to shovel every inch of snow before we can flood the rink again. We'll do it after school."

Jesse headed to the pay phone and dialed home to get his mother's permission. She said she would pick him up at Jonathan's house at five o'clock.

During recess and lunch the boys practiced their shepherd lines, and that afternoon at the dress rehearsal they didn't miss a single one.

Mr. O'Donnell was full of compliments. "And your costumes are great, guys, and your staffs are terrific!" He stuck his thumb in the air. "You make a very convincing pair of shepherds. Wow!"

At the end of the school day the boys were so pleased with themselves they almost floated over the snow to Jonathan's house. They burst through the back door, proclaiming the exact words Mr. O'Donnell had spoken.

They discovered Mr. Agnew in the living room, staring vacantly at the TV.

He looked over at the boys, but didn't say a word. Even when Jonathan repeated all the great things Mr. O'Donnell had said.

"Dad, you gotta see the concert."

His father shook his head. He turned back to the TV.

Jesse's eye caught a half-carved piece of wood cast aside on the coffee table.

Later, outside, the boys had little heart for shoveling.

Jonathan sat on a snowbank and looked miserable. "And I thought things were going to get better."

"Everything takes time," Jesse said. "He needs to give it another try."

"What's the use?"

At five o'clock, after he and Jonathan had made another halfhearted attempt at shoveling, Jesse's mother drove up. As Jesse climbed into the car Jonathan turned and headed inside without even saying good-bye.

On their way home Jesse told his mother the whole story.

"What can we do?" he asked when they were in the house and sitting on the sofa.

"I don't know. Jonathan's dad is a stubborn man. Sure doesn't sound like he's about to change."

His mother was standing by the mantel, next to a new Santa. Jesse hardly paid him any attention.

She held him up in her hands. "So," she said, "in the House of Wooden Santas . . . "

But Jesse had a lot more on his mind. "Maybe . . . if we wished for it . . . "

"What?"

JOY

"I got it. Maybe, instead of presents for Christmas, what we wished for was Mr. Agnew to smarten up."

Jesse's mother stared at him. "I don't know about that. . . . "

"Sure, you're the one who said all that stuff about trust. You're the one who said you got to search it out and hold onto it."

"But this is a lot to ask."

"Forget it, then," he blurted.

"Now, Jesse."

"You make up all these dumb stories about Santa Claus! And now you say there's nothing he can do!"

"I didn't say that."

"And that proves he's not real!"

"I think he *would* help. . . . "

"Okay, then. Prove it."

There was a long period of silence when Jesse knew his mom was staring at him. He wouldn't look back.

She laid Santa in his lap. Jesse wouldn't look at him *or* his mother.

"In the House of Wooden Santas we gotta learn to get along."

"Not my fault."

"This old fellow doesn't like it when we argue. Especially over him."

Jesse pressed his lips together.

"He could be *Wish Santa.*"

"Yeah, right," Jesse muttered.

"You wish for what you want. And I'll wish for peace between us. Whaddya say?"

Jesse thought about it, but he didn't say anything.

His mother wouldn't take her eyes off him. "What have we got to lose?"

Jesse took Santa in his hands and held him out in front of them.

"Okay, Mr. Santa. I made a wish. Whaddya going to do about it?"

THIRTEEN DAYS TO CHRISTMAS

It was the big day, the day of the concert.

His mother would be there, of course, and Jonathan's mom.

At the final rehearsal Jonathan's mind seemed miles away.

"That night," said Jonathan, "we were in the fields, keeping watch over our folks. . . . "

"Flocks, Jonathan, *flocks,"* interrupted Mr. O'Donnell. He scowled at him.

"It's okay, sir," Jesse stammered. "He'll be perfect tonight."

"The whole class is counting on you guys."

"We won't let anyone down."

Jesse cornered Jonathan in the hallway after the school bell. "You can't mess up tonight with all those people in the audience, all those mothers and fathers. . . . "

Jesse twisted his mouth, but he couldn't take back what had slipped out.

"I know," Jonathan said.

"You got to concentrate."

"Sure," Jonathan muttered and wandered off.

Jesse could do nothing. Nothing except hope.

At least they would have luck on their side. If he could believe his mother, they would. When Jesse arrived home that afternoon, she popped out of her workroom, holding another Santa.

"Ladies and gentlemen. Tonight, riding through the House of Wooden Santas, I present to you . . . someone every performer needs — *Good Luck Santa!* He carries a horseshoe, a rabbit's paw, a shiny penny. So, go ahead, rub his head for good luck."

Jesse brushed his hand over the curve of wood.

"Ta-da!" exclaimed his mother.

She whisked Santa into a box.

"Show's over, I'm afraid." She crumpled up newspaper and stuffed it around him. "I made a wish that this old fellow will bring us *both* good luck. Maybe our Santas will finally start to sell. Christmas Day is less than two weeks away."

As soon as supper was over they were in the car, off to the concert. All the way there Jesse practiced his lines, making sure he hadn't forgotten any of them. He hoped Jonathan was doing the same.

But when he arrived in school, he found it wasn't lines that Jonathan had forgotten.

He was in his shepherd's costume, standing in front of Mr. O'Donnell. Without a staff in his hand.

"Jonathan, how did you . . . ?"

"I just did, sir."

"But it was part of your costume. And all that work your father did."

"I know, sir. I'm sorry."

Mr. O'Donnell walked away, shaking his head.

Theirs was the last item on the program.

A light shone above a wooden stable in the center of the stage. The boys walked slowly up the aisle from the back of the gym, two shepherds leading the angels, the animals, and the Wise Men. In their midst was Mary and Joseph and the Child. The rest of the class surrounded the stable, singing, "O Little Town of Bethlehem."

Jesse spied his mother and gave her a smile as he walked by. Reverend Agnew was sitting next to her. But there was no sign of Jonathan's dad.

Jesse glanced at Jonathan. No staff. No smile. Not a glimmer of hope his father would show up. Pretty sad-looking for a shepherd.

The procession gathered inside the stable, just as the carol ended. Jesse looked into the audience.

There was Jonathan's dad!

Now Jonathan saw him, too, sure enough, making his way slowly up a side aisle. Jonathan's staff was in his hand.

He encountered Jonathan's teacher and handed him the staff. Mr. O'Donnell made his way to the stable and quickly passed it to Jonathan.

Jonathan broke into a smile. His dad raised a hand to him, and Jonathan gave him a wave with his staff.

It was time to begin the narration. The two shepherds took turns telling the story of the Birth, with the others in the stable each delivering a line when the shepherds mentioned them by name. All except for the Child. To the Child the choir sang "Silent Night" with the whole school joining in on the final verse.

Neither Jonathan nor Jesse had missed a line. Their voices were as strong and clear as Mr. O'Donnell had ever wanted them to be. The audience clapped and clapped. Just as the curtain was closing, Jonathan waved to his dad once again.

In the midst of all the excitement, Jesse was thinking about his own dad, that some day he might show up at a Christmas concert.

Later, when the boys had changed out of their costumes and made their way to where the parents were waiting, Jonathan was all smiles. His dad put his hand on his shoulder.

"You did great."

"You changed your mind," Jonathan said.

"After you and your mother had gone, I saw the staff standing there. When I took hold of it I started to think about when I was your age, when I had a part in a Christmas concert. I guess I really wanted to see you on that stage."

"Thanks a lot, Dad."

"It was worth it. Best pair of shepherds I ever saw."

Jesse's mother insisted they all come to their house. They ended up, the five of them, around the kitchen table, a pot of tea and a pile of toast in the center.

"A fine way to end the day," Jesse's mother declared.

"Are you shepherds available on the twenty-fourth?" Jonathan's mother asked all of a sudden. "I'm sure there must be some way to fit you into our Christmas Eve service at church."

Jonathan and Jesse looked at each other. They didn't have to think about it twice.

"Wicked!" said Jonathan.

"Could you come up with a word that's a bit more . . . suitable?" Reverend Agnew's face was as twisted as if she had bitten into a lemon.

"Awesome?" Jesse said.

"Wild?" Jonathan said.

"I was thinking more along the lines of . . . wondrous."

"Guys," Jonathan's father said, "that's what shepherds are. Wild and woolly and *wondrous!*"

TWELVE DAYS TO CHRISTMAS

"So," said his mother when Jesse appeared at the door of the workroom, "Jonathan's dad showed up at the concert. Santa came through in the crunch."

"Think my wish really had anything to do with that?"

"Helped, I'd say. Wouldn't you?"

Jesse walked into the room, thinking hard about it.

His mother had let him sleep in because he had been so late getting to bed the night before. "I called Mr. O'Donnell," she said. "We had a long chat. He's a nice man. I let him know you wouldn't be in school until this afternoon."

Jesse loved surprises. His mother had another one for him.

"How would you like to do some painting for me?"

She had never suggested such a thing before. Jesse thought he could never be of much help, although he had sometimes painted ornaments for their Christmas tree.

She took a figure out of the cabinet behind her and placed him on the table. He was bare, unpainted wood. He looked like he was about to fly.

"This guy could do with some color on his cloak," his mother said. She laid out a clean brush and a small pot of scarlet paint.

Jesse had never seen such a Santa. He began in earnest to paint the fellow's cloak, while his mother sketched on paper some things she might put in his hands.

Jesse loved it — he and his mom working together, school far off, Christmas so near.

The doorbell rang.

His mother went to answer it, leaving Jesse hard at work. But his brushstrokes came to a sudden stop. He heard the bark of a dog. And a voice that put a knot in his stomach.

He set aside the brush and peered down the hall. There, standing beside his mother, was Mrs. Wentzell — and Ivan in her arms.

The dog yapped at Jesse. The voices fell silent. Jesse's mother walked back to him.

"That's okay, love. You finish what you were doing."

Jesse returned to his painting. His mother closed the door.

Something was up. He put his ear to the door. He couldn't make out what they were saying. He eased the door open just a crack.

"You can't do this," his mother said, her words quick and anxious. "I should have the money soon."

"I think I've given you more than enough time," said Mrs. Wentzell. "I would like you out of the house by the first of January."

"It's Christmas."

"I'm sorry."

"And we couldn't possibly find another place around here."

"I'm sure you won't have to go far."

And with that Mrs. Wentzell was gone.

It was minutes before Jesse's mother returned to the workroom. She didn't look at Jesse. But he could see how angry she was.

Jesse kept it in for as long as he could, then broke into tears.

"Hey, no need of that. We'll figure out something," his mother said. She put an arm around him.

"How did she get to be such a crab?!"

"Who knows?"

Jesse dried his eyes. People had no right to be like that! Especially at Christmas.

Jesse went back to his painting. With every stroke of the brush he was more and more determined to figure out something that would make Mrs. Wentzell change her mind.

Jonathan's father had changed his mind. Sure enough.

Maybe he and Santa — and maybe Jonathan, the three of them together — could come up with something that would work on the crab, too.

"You like this place now, I guess," his mother said, trying to be her regular self.

"Maybe."

She caught his eye. There appeared on his face the barest hint of a smile. It met her own sluggish one.

"Maybe Santa Claus will help us."

Her smile widened a bit. "Really?"

"Yeah, why not?" said Jesse, sounding tough about it all.

She picked up Santa Claus and held him in the air with one hand. She had him flying over the table.

"From out of the sky, swooping into the House of Wooden Santas," she said in a voice too dreary. She turned up the volume and tried to add some spark to it. "With fire in his eyes and passion in his heart! Is it a bird? Is it a plane?"

"No," shouted Jesse, "it's *Super Santa!*"

"He's decided to scour the world for crabby people who don't know the meaning of Christmas!"

"But this guy doesn't look much like a super hero," said Jesse. "His cloak is too heavy."

"The woodworker will just have to work her woodworking magic. She can chip away to reveal a *Super Santa* suit. She can shape a few muscles. She can shed a few pounds."

Jesse was feeling a lot better.

"Now watch as I begin by turning his scarlet cloak into a Christmas cape."

Jesse's mom, chisel in hand, started the transformation.

It took several hours, and Jesse had to go off to school before *Super Santa* was complete.

But that night, when his mother flew the fellow into Jesse's room, he was every inch a super hero.

Jesse lay in bed, his hands behind his head, and stared at him and wondered how in the world they could ever transform the heart of Mrs. Wentzell. It might not be easy.

Jesse remembered the look Mrs. Wentzell had given him in church on Sunday.

It might be next to impossible.

ELEVEN DAYS TO CHRISTMAS

"Nothing's impossible," Jonathan said after school that day.

They were standing on top of a snowbank, looking down on a sheet of water turning into a sheet of ice.

"You thought *this* would be impossible, didn't you?" he said to Jesse.

"Well . . . "

"Well, tomorrow we skate."

"And the next day we fly!" exclaimed Jesse. "Like Santa!"

"I don't think so."

They plopped down on the snowbank. Neither of them said a word for a long time.

"Maybe if we went to her house and . . . " Jonathan couldn't think of anything else.

"Maybe if we phoned her or wrote her a letter," said Jesse.

"What would we say?"

"That she can't do this. We all got rights. That nobody can be *that* mean."

The more Jesse thought about it, the more he figured it would never work. They dragged themselves into Jonathan's house.

"So down in the mouth," said Jonathan's father when they had gotten rid of their winter clothes and had sunk into the living room sofa. Jesse couldn't tell whether he was being funny or serious. There was an odd kind of shyness in the way he was looking at them.

"Got something to show you," he said.

The boys followed him through a back door to the garage. Standing on an old table, surrounded by wood chips, was a carving. The boys looked at it, then at each other.

The carving was bigger and rougher than anything Jesse's mother would have done, and it wasn't painted, but there was no mistaking what it was.

"He's us," Jonathan said.

It was a carving of a shepherd boy carrying a staff. He looked like Jonathan or Jesse on the night of the concert.

"Maybe I'll try another one," his father said. "And have a pair of them. Think I should?"

It was the first time Jesse had ever seen Jonathan's father pleased with himself.

"Cool," Jonathan said.

"Wondrous," Jesse said.

The other two laughed.

"I gotta tell Mom," said Jonathan. "She'll go nuts. And your mother."

Before long he was back, dragging both of them from Reverend Agnew's office.

"Wow!"

"It *is* good. I mean it," said Jesse's mom.

"He never told me a thing," said Reverend Agnew. "I suspected he was up to something, but I wouldn't dare ask what it was."

"He's going to do another one," Jonathan announced proudly.

Jesse's mom clenched a fist. "Terrific."

When Jesse and his mom left for home she was sounding cheerier than she had all day.

"Got to look on the bright side," she said, pulling into their driveway.

As she unlocked the front door, the telephone rang. She kicked off her boots and scurried to get to it, calling back, "Could be worse, you know."

Jesse crashed on the living room sofa. The Christmas decorations seemed to hang limp. What would be the fun of Christmas if right after it they would have to pack up everything and take off and never ever see this place again?

His mother walked into the living room and stood over him. Her arms were folded, and her lips tight together. Her eyes widened.

"It *is* worse," she said.

Jesse sat up and she sat next to him.

"That was the craft shop." She put an arm around his shoulders. "They *thought* they had sold two of the Santas."

Jesse's head fell against his mother.

"A man bought one, then returned it for a refund. His wife didn't like it. Wanted something with real velvet and lace."

"Puke," Jesse said.

"Wasn't fancy enough for her furniture."

"Gross."

"Someone else put one on hold. Never showed up again."

"What a dummy!"

His mother built a fire in the fireplace. They ate pizza in front of it and listened to Christmas music.

"There's no need to worry," she insisted.

Jesse lay on the sofa and slowly sank into a daydream world of other Christmases. His mother covered him with a quilt.

Later that evening, through heavy eyelids, he saw his mother bring in a figure and put him on the mantel. Santa sat with his legs hanging over the edge, his ankles crossed.

Jesse's mother sat on the floor beside the sofa. She whispered, "In the House of Wooden Santas sits *Santa of Times Past.* He's our memory of better days, when we knew for sure what each Christmas would bring."

Jesse heard faint strains of his mother's voice, soft verses of a song, the one about a white Christmas.

Later the doorbell rang. It broke Jesse's sleep. He heard the voice of his teacher.

He did not move. Just opened one eye from time to time.

"Sorry if I startled you," Jesse heard him say.

"You didn't really, Mr. O'Donnell," answered his mother.

"Keith," he said. "I belong to a local service club. We do what we can this time of the year for those families that might use a little help. We're distributing some Christmas hampers. Thought you and Jesse might like one."

"No, thank you."

"It's just people helping each other, quietly doing what we can."

"I would prefer we pay our own way, Mr. O'Donn . . . Keith."

"I understand. It's just that Christmas can be an expensive time for a lot of people. It's just to ease the load a bit."

Jesse heard the crunch of snow. A long time passed without a sound.

Jesse heard the crunch of snow again. He saw Mr. O'Donnell walk down the hallway, a heavy box in his hands. There was a thud on the kitchen floor.

"Would you like a coffee?" his mother said.

"I'd love one."

Jesse could hear their voices in the kitchen. His teacher talked about his work. Jesse's mother talked about hers.

"I'd love to see one of the Santas . . . if you wouldn't mind."

His mother tiptoed into the living room. Jesse shut both eyes. He opened one again as she was leaving. She had Santa in her hand.

"Gee," Mr. O'Donnell said. "And it's all carved by hand?"

"Machines that can do this work are a little hard to come by."

"Sorry."

"That's okay."

"It's wonderful."

"Thank you."

"How much would you charge? I mean, are they expensive?"

She told him the price. There was a long pause in the conversation.

"A lot of work involved, as you can see."

"Of course."

Another pause.

Then Jesse heard the crumple of newspaper.

He saw Mr. O'Donnell pass down the hallway, carrying a shoebox. Saw his mother standing there, waiting for Mr. O'Donnell to leave.

Saw in her hand a clump of money.

TEN DAYS TO CHRISTMAS

When Jesse woke he was in his bed. But something was weird. Something was missing.

He sat at the kitchen table, blurry-eyed, his hair bent in all directions. One look at his mother and he remembered.

"Where's the guy for yesterday?"

His mother smiled. "Sold. Gone. Out the door. Money in the pocket."

Jesse stared at her. "Really?" he said, trying to sound surprised.

"Called him *Santa of Times Past.* Reminded me of the Christmases we used to have."

"Who bought him?" As if he didn't know already.

"Your teacher. Last night. Must have heard about my carving. He came by . . . when you were asleep . . . asked to see a Santa. Bought him right there on the spot."

Jesse looked away and finished his breakfast.

"The big number one. This is the start. I can feel it in my bones."

Jesse didn't know what he was feeling in his bones.

All during school that day Mr. O'Donnell kept giving him odd looks, as if he knew he wasn't paying attention, just pretending to.

"Jesse," he said, after the bell had gone that afternoon. "So . . . your mother carves Santas."

"Yes, sir."

"Think she might come to class and talk about it? There's only five school days until Christmas holidays, and I was thinking . . . what can we do this year for a special treat?"

"Probably she would, sir."

"Don't think she'd mind," said Jonathan. "She showed my dad. And my dad is very stubborn."

Mr. O'Donnell smiled, as if his whole world had brightened. "Fabulous."

As Jesse and Jonathan were leaving, he called out, "Maybe I'll phone her at home. If that's okay. Or drop by your house later. If that's okay."

"Sure."

"That's what I'll do then. I'll drop by. Just for a few minutes. Okay. Perfect." Mr. O'Donnell's smile was bigger than ever.

As the boys left the school, Jonathan said what was on both their minds. "Mr. O'Donnell can be very weird sometimes."

Jesse spied his bus. "See ya," he said. "Tomorrow. Top secret meeting." Then he added in a heavy whisper. "O.W. — Operation Wentzell."

"Got it."

At home Jesse found his mother in her usual spot in her workroom.

"Mr. O'Donnell said he might come by later."

She put down her paintbrush.

"Really?"

Jesse was sure there was excitement in her voice. He looked at her very intently.

"What for?" she asked.

"Who knows?"

She glared at him. "Jesse . . . "

He wouldn't say a word.

She growled and threatened to pounce on him.

He ran off. His mother scurried out from behind the table and chased after him. He raced to his room and fumbled at the door to lock it, but he wasn't fast enough. His mother forced her way in. She just about nabbed him when he squirmed away and darted off again.

Out through the kitchen and into the living room, around the sofa, and back down the hallway, around and around, laughing and yelling at each other all the time. Once he slipped and fell flat on his rear.

He thought for sure she had caught him. But he wormed through her legs, screaming wildly.

Finally she collapsed on the sofa. "I give up!"

The doorbell rang.

"Oh, no . . . "

She tried desperately to get her breath back and look normal.

"Jesse," she called. "It's him. He'll think we're crazy."

Jesse appeared and sagged to the floor, exhausted. "You answer it."

"You."

"No, you."

There was a loud knock.

Jesse and his mother dragged themselves to the door together.

"Hi, Keith . . . Mr. O'Donnell," his mother said. Out sputtered a laugh.

Jesse gave her a hard look.

"Sorry. We were playing chase. It was very funny."

Mr. O'Donnell seemed rather bewildered.

"He wants you to come to school," Jesse said.

His teacher nodded. "To talk to the class about your work. If you're not too busy, that is."

She looked at Jesse and then Mr. O'Donnell. She shrugged. "Sure, why not."

"Great."

"Anything for a laugh." She started to chuckle, but nobody else cracked a smile. "Sorry. I've been in a silly mood all day."

Mr. O'Donnell set a date for Thursday afternoon and left.

"Good-bye," Jesse's mother called as he reached his car. "So long. See you then. Cheerio."

She closed the door and fell against it, and broke out laughing once again.

"Mom, you're cracked."

"I haven't had such a good laugh in months."

"And now Mr. O'Donnell knows you're cracked."

"Did I embarrass you?"

"Yes."

"Oh, well." She covered her mouth with her hand to hold the laughter in.

When she had wiped her eyes for the final time she wrapped an arm around Jesse and dragged him into her workroom. She grabbed the newest Santa with her free hand.

All three of them fell to the living room sofa in a heap, Santa on top.

"A day should never go by without a chuckle, eh, *Jolly Ol' Santa?* No matter what. That's why I invited you to this crazy House of Wooden Santas, right? To keep us laughing."

She handed him over to Jesse.

"He'll put the merry in your Christmas and the happy in your New Year!" Laughter bubbled inside her, then burst out.

"Cracked," Jesse said.

She placed Santa carefully on an end table. "Ummmm . . . "

She raised her hand and wriggled her fingers over Jesse. Before he could squirm away she got him in the ribs.

All he could do was laugh and laugh and howl and laugh.

NINE DAYS TO CHRISTMAS

"Jonathan says not to forget your skates," Jesse's mother called out to him. She had just hung up the telephone.

Jesse looked out his bedroom window. The frost overnight had made wonderful patterns on the glass. His eyes traced the crystal swirls.

Sunshine flooded the world outside. The snow gleamed. Jesse could see smoke rising straight up from the houses at the end of the road.

Jesse dug out his skates from the back of the closet. He sat on the corner of the bed for a while, looking them over. He touched the blades with his thumb. They were still sharp. It brought back the memory of his best goal ever, that time he deked the goalie on a breakaway and scored to win that play-off game.

He put the skate guards on the blades, tied the laces together, and slung the skates over his shoulder. It would be good just to have them on his feet again.

The rink wasn't nearly as bad as he had imagined it. The ice was rough in places, and he couldn't build up any speed like he loved to do, but it was crazy fun to take a flying leap into a snowbank and lie there under the sky, the snowflakes drifting around him, and his breath billowing out in clouds.

Of course he loved the fact that he scored tons of goals on Jonathan. When two other boys saw them having so much fun, they showed up with their skates and the four of them made teams. Jesse and Jonathan were the Leafs, and right then and there they played the final game for the Stanley Cup, and of course the Leafs won!

They celebrated the first day on the rink with Mr. Agnew's pea soup and dumplings. Jonathan ate three bowls of it. And Jesse, even though he never liked soup much, finished off a second helping. His mother showed up with a plateful of cookies just as they finished — raspberry jam-jams, still warm.

"When I was a little girl my mother would make these every Christmas," she said.

"Deadly," said Jonathan, and scooped up another one.

Reverend Agnew smiled. "Doesn't Christmas make you long to be a child again? The sounds, the glimpses of secrets that made you so excited you couldn't sleep?"

Jesse's mother said, "I remember getting a letter from Santa Claus. . . . "

Jesse had been sitting through it all without saying a word. But the more they talked, the more excited he became. It was building up a fantastic idea in his head.

He couldn't stand it any longer. He dragged Jonathan away to the basement, pretending he had to show him some new hockey move.

Jonathan grabbed his stick, but Jesse took it out of his hand and led him to a corner of the basement, where there was no chance they could be heard.

"I don't get it," said Jonathan.

"I got this brain wave," said Jesse. "I got a way to make Mrs. Wentzell change her mind."

They slapped each other's hand as if they had just scored a goal.

"How?" said Jonathan.

"We get her in the Christmas spirit, like she must have been when she was a little girl. Then she'll have to change her mind. Remember: 'Peace on earth and goodwill to men.'"

"And women," said Jonathan. "But what if she's been crabby all her life?"

"C'mon. Nobody can be that bad."

Jonathan was thinking. "You're right," he said. "There's nobody who doesn't try to be at least a bit good this time of the year . . . just in case." Then he added, "Okay, where do we start?"

"First thing we do is scout out her house. Then we start making plans."

"You mean Operation Wentzell goes into action?"

"Right."

"Now?"

"Right. Now."

They left the house with a secret mission. They were supposed to be going to the convenience store to spend some of Jonathan's allowance, but what they were really doing was going to the store, spending the money, *and* scouting out the Wentzell house. It was up a side road, not far from the store.

As it came in sight, they took to the woods and approached it under cover of some pine trees. They chewed long shoestrings of red licorice and took careful note of every important detail about the house.

"Chimney," said Jesse.

"That means fireplace."

"No wreath on front door."

"That means doesn't like Christmas visitors."

"No Christmas lights on tree in front yard."

"That means hates Christmas."

The boys were secretly hoping Mrs. Wentzell would come out the front door and pass right by without seeing them, but they had no such luck.

On the way back to Jonathan's house they tried to figure out what they would do with all the information they had gathered so far.

"If . . . " Jesse started, but gave up. He summoned new courage. "If she's going to get the Christmas spirit, then the first thing she's got to do is believe in Santa Claus."

Jonathan didn't say anything.

"Right?"

"I guess so."

Jesse looked him in the eye.

"What if there isn't one?" Jonathan said weakly.

"What if there *is?"* Jesse snapped back. If everyone had to see everything before they could believe in it, then nobody would believe in God, either."

"I know that."

"This could be your test," said Jesse. "If Mrs. Wentzell gets the Christmas spirit and changes her mind, then there is a Santa Claus."

"If she doesn't, there's not?"

"Exactly."

"Wicked," said Jonathan.

The boys paused for a minute, as if they needed time for it all to sink in.

"So how do we get Mrs. Wentzell into the Christmas spirit?" Jonathan asked.

"For that we go to the guy himself."

"Santa Claus?"

"Yep."

Jonathan stared at Jesse. He didn't get it.

"You gotta have trust," said Jesse. "That's what my mother says."

That night Jesse sat on the sofa and studied his mother's newest Santa for the clues he was looking for.

"In the House of Wooden Santas . . . " said his mother.

"Wait."

She looked at him curiously.

"I'm trying to concentrate," said Jesse.

He ignored his mother and stared at the wooden figure. She left the room and went into the kitchen.

"In the House of Wooden Santas . . . " Jesse began.

"Hey," said his mother as she came back in the room, sipping a mug of tea, "that's my line."

"Shhhh . . . " With a finger to his lips Jesse continued, " . . . is a Santa who is trying to tell me something. He's saying . . . "

Jesse closed his eyes and concentrated even harder.

"He's saying . . . I am *Santa of Family and Friends.* She has never forgotten their good times together. In this sack are the memories. Dig them out. See them, hear them, feel them. . . . "

His mother kissed him and exclaimed, "You came up with that all by yourself. You're *so* precious."

Jesse opened his eyes.

He was a bit stunned for the moment. "I had help," he stammered.

He really did. It was as if Santa had put a staff in his hand and pointed him to the sack. In the sack he found what he was looking for.

His mother was smiling broadly.

Jesse didn't have the heart to tell her. But his mother wasn't really the "she" he and Santa were talking about. Nope, the sack had to be opened for someone else.

And tomorrow he and Jonathan would be the ones to open it. And start the digging.

EIGHT DAYS TO CHRISTMAS

As soon as church was over that morning, Jesse made a beeline for Jonathan. The two of them squeezed ahead of everyone else, down the stairs to the basement of the church. They went straight to the chocolate cupcakes, then hurried off to a corner by themselves.

"Mrs. Wentzell wasn't in church this morning," said Jesse.

"She's probably home thinking up new ways to be crabby," grunted Jonathan.

"She won't be for long."

Jesse told him excitedly how he and Santa had come up with the answer he was looking for.

"Really?" Jonathan said, looking more than a little confused. "But what does it all mean?"

"It means," said Jesse, "the first question we got to ask ourselves is: What is the most exciting thing that could ever happen to her at this time of the year?"

Jonathan started to think about it.

"Got it," said Jesse, who had done a lot of his thinking beforehand. "Getting a letter directly from old Santa himself."

"Exactly what I was going to say," Jonathan mumbled through a mouthful of cupcake.

They finished off their cupcakes, feeling very pleased with themselves. Jesse began looking about for his mother.

"She's talking to someone," Jonathan said. "It's Mr. O'Donnell." On their way over to them Jonathan whispered in Jesse's ear, "Never saw him in church before."

"A pair of shepherds, is it?" Mr. O'Donnell said, bright and cheery.

"Hello, sir," the boys answered in unison.

"Mom, I really need to go over to Jonathan's after lunch."

"We'll see."

"Ple-e-ease," said Jesse. "I have to."

"It's okay," said Jonathan. "My dad will be home. He won't mind."

Mr. O'Donnell turned even brighter. "This sounds promising."

Jesse's mom started to say something and stopped. She started again. "Mr. O'Donnell has invited me to go snowshoeing with him this afternoon."

Jesse was stunned. "Really? In the woods?"

He just couldn't picture his teacher and his mother in the woods together. With big clumpy snowshoes on their feet.

"By yourselves?" he said.

"I think we better be going, Jesse." His mother put her arm around him and led him away. "Jonathan, your mom is probably looking for you."

They left Mr. O'Donnell standing there, drinking his coffee alone. "I'll see you later?" he said.

Nobody answered him. Jesse's mom gave him a weak smile.

"Weird," Jonathan whispered in Jesse's ear and took off.

Jesse and his mother were in the car and halfway home before either of them spoke. Finally Jesse couldn't hold it in any longer. "A fellow's mom doesn't go snowshoeing with his teacher. Especially Mr. O'Donnell."

His mother laughed.

But she wasn't agreeing with him.

"Weird," Jesse said.

"He *was* acting rather strange. But he *is* nice."

"For a teacher." Now Jesse was very confused.

He didn't want to talk about it anymore. There was enough craziness in his life already. Why the heck did his mother have to add some more?

When his mother called him to lunch Jesse found a Santa in the center of the table. He ignored him.

He ate without a word.

"The silent treatment," said his mother. "Haven't seen that one for . . . must be at least a week."

Jesse growled under his breath.

During dessert she started to hum, then chant, "In the House of Wooden Santas . . . *Music Santa* stands, not saying a word. Just playing his music."

Jesse pressed his lips together. He was determined not to find it one bit funny.

"Wonder what he's playing? 'Silent Night' maybe. Maybe it's 'O Come, All Ye Speechless.'"

Jesse pressed his lips together even more tightly. But his lips couldn't stand the pressure, and out sputtered a laugh.

"Santa knows," said his mother, "that silence can make beautiful music."

Jesse rolled his eyes.

Oh no, he thought, now she's going to sing. So he jumped up from the table and went for his coat and mitts.

"Okay, let's go!" he shouted.

Finally she drove him to Jonathan's house. As he was getting out of the car, she said, "Maybe I won't go with Mr. O'Donnell."

Jesse turned back. "Go if you want to go, but don't talk about me. And don't get in one of your goofy moods."

With that he was gone. He ran up the path and into the house. He escaped inside without even ringing the doorbell.

"Jonathan!" he called out.

"Come on up!" Jonathan yelled from the top of the stairs.

Jonathan had a pencil and paper and an envelope all set out on his desk. He had also done some investigation in his mother's office and found out Mrs. Wentzell's first name.

It took a while and a pile of crumpled-up balls of their rough copies, but eventually they had their letter. Jesse read it aloud as one final check.

Dear Little Alma:

I hope you have been a good little girl this year. Have you?! I know that sometimes it is hard to be nice to people, but remember that Santa only comes to good girls and not nasty ones. If you haven't been good, there is still time before Christmas Day. If you don't try, there'll be a wondrous big lump of coal for you.

Lots of love, Santa.

Jonathan had drawn a picture of Santa with a speech balloon that read: *Santa's watching you. Ho! Ho! Ho!*

"This should get her in the Christmas spirit," said Jonathan.

"Maybe Santa sounds a bit tough," Jesse said.

So they decided to add a P. S. to the letter. It read: *If you turn out to be a real good girl, Santa will fill your stocking to the very brim.*

And with that they folded the letter and put it in an envelope. Jonathan printed *Little Alma* on the front of it.

When they approached her house later that afternoon, with the envelope safely tucked inside Jesse's coat, they found her driveway empty.

"Great," declared Jonathan.

He kept watch on the road while Jesse ran to the front door.

Jesse slyly drew out the envelope, looking all around as he did. He tried pushing it under the door but there was no space. He tried wedging it between the handle and the door frame, but it kept slipping away.

"Car!" Jonathan shouted, scampering into the trees.

Jesse darted about, trying to find some place to leave it. Finally he dropped it on the doorstep. He quickly made a snowball and plopped it on top of the envelope so it would not blow away.

He raced into the trees. Jonathan pulled him down flat to the snow.

Mrs. Wentzell's car turned into the driveway.

They peered through the trees as she walked from the car to her front door. Her eyes fell on the envelope.

She picked it up and brushed away the bits of snow still clinging to it. She seemed to have trouble reading the words.

Her head straightened up quickly. She looked all around.

Jesse and Jonathan snapped their heads out of sight.

They slowly lifted them up again. Mrs. Wentzell had gone inside, the front door closed behind her.

Jesse could only stare at the door and imagine the joy on her face and the warm glow filling her heart.

"First stage, Operation Wentzell . . . complete," Jonathan announced.

"Santa alert, Santa alert!" Jesse proclaimed.

SEVEN DAYS TO CHRISTMAS

"Outside the House of Wooden Santas . . . " Jesse's mother began, the first thing in the morning, smiling broadly from across the kitchen, " . . . some fellow's heard the call of the wild."

She howled a little, like a young wolf.

Okay, thought Jesse, what's up now? He gave his mother a sharp, eagle eye.

She howled a little more. "This woodsman is wild about nature. He knows every bird and beast by name. He can spot a partridge at a hundred yards. He can snowshoe better than the snowshoe hare."

Yeah, now I get it, Jesse said to himself.

On the kitchen counter was the red wool toque his mother had been wearing the day before. She held it upright by its tassel. "Here he is . . . " and she howled again just as she whipped the toque up from the counter, *"Santa of the Wilds!"*

"Mom," Jesse said with a growling whine.

His mother grinned mischievously.

At school that morning Jesse came face to face with Mr. O'Donnell acting even more strangely than his mother. During the opening announcements Mr. O'Donnell looked as if his mind was in the clouds, floating around the classroom. When it landed on Jesse, it came with a long, bright-eyed smile that reminded Jesse of an overgrown elf.

Each time his teacher looked at him, Jesse couldn't help but think of his mother and Mr. O'Donnell tramping through the woods on snowshoes.

When Jesse arrived back home his mother was hard at work. He poked his head in her room. "Heard anything from Mrs. Wentzell? Do we still have to get out of the house?"

His mother dropped her paintbrush and looked at him with suspicion. "Are you up to something?"

"I was just wondering . . . if she called . . . maybe."

His mother's eyes filled with concern. "No, dear."

Jesse left before she had chance to ask any questions.

He phoned Jonathan right away. "No word. Nothing," he told him.

There was a lot of grumbling and then a long silence.

"Guess we need a stage two," said Jesse finally.

"Guess so. Dad said she's a tough nut."

They chuckled a little.

"Time to bring out the nutcracker," Jonathan said.

They chuckled a little more.

"Wow!" said Jesse.

"What?" said Jonathan.

"Nutcracker. Get it? Santa's magic must still be at work in my head. Wow. . . . "

"What? You mean . . . "

"Sugar plum fairies and all that."

"Operation Wentzell, stage two?"

"Exactly."

They worked out a plan. That night Jesse would call up Mrs. Wentzell, and as soon as she answered he would play music from *The Nutcracker* over the phone. They each looked up Mrs. Wentzell's number in the phone book, and when they agreed they had the right one, Jesse wrote it on his hand.

"I can see her dancing now!"

"A little girl again," Jesse said, "dancing with the spirit of Christmas!"

They could hardly wait.

After supper Jesse went straight to clearing away the table and running the water for his mother to wash the dishes.

"You're being very helpful tonight," she said, suspicion still in her voice.

"I know you're anxious to get back to work." He looked at her as if she were acting strangely for no reason.

Jesse set out his school books on the kitchen table and started his homework. The second his mother went into her workroom he called out, "Okay if I put on some Christmas music?"

"That would be lovely. Turn it up loud enough that I can hear."

From his jeans pocket he plucked a tape with "The Dance of the Sugarplum Fairy" on it. He slipped it into the boom box on the kitchen counter. He had to wait out "The Twelve Days of Christmas," which seemed to go on and on forever. Finally, with the twelve lords a-leaping, Jesse turned up the music a couple of notches, then dialed Mrs. Wentzell's number. All but the last digit.

As soon as the sugarplum fairy took over, he hit the final number on the phone. He held the receiver close to his ear, but not so close it would block out the music.

Someone picked up the phone. A dog was yapping in the background. "Hello." Definitely Mrs. Wentzell.

Jesse held the receiver in the air and as near to the boom box as the cord would stretch. He couldn't help but do a little sugarplum dance, just as he imagined Mrs. Wentzell was doing in her own kitchen that very second.

"Jesse!" The yell of his mother from her workroom.

Jesse stared at the receiver in his outstretched hand! He ran to the phone and banged the receiver back in place.

"Jesse, turn the music down! It's too loud. How can you concentrate on your homework?"

He couldn't, not now.

The telephone rang.

Mrs. Wentzell?! He panicked. "Mom!" he yelled. "Could you get that! I gotta go, bad."

He ran to the bathroom, locked the door, and sat on the toilet cover, in dread of what might come next.

"Jesse, it's for you."

Jesse winced.

"It's Jonathan."

"I'll be right there."

He flushed the toilet, then hurried to the phone.

His mother held out the receiver. "That's quick. You don't look well. You don't have diarrhea, do you?"

"Mom . . . " He took the receiver.

Jonathan was laughing.

"It's not funny," Jesse groaned.

It was several minutes after his mother finally drifted back into her workroom before Jesse could whisper to him about his rotten luck with Mrs. Wentzell.

"Maybe she didn't hear."

"Maybe she's deaf. Yeah, right."

"Maybe she hung up before it happened."

"Either way, it was a disaster."

There was glum silence.

"Guess we'll just have to figure on a stage three," said Jonathan.

More glum silence.

SIX DAYS TO CHRISTMAS

Stage three took place in the freezing cold outside Mrs. Wentzell's.

Jonathan tried to be funny by calling it stage "tree" because of the fir tree that stood in Mrs. Wentzell's front yard, but he wasn't laughing much.

Jesse was especially serious because he had just spent all his money, the money he had been saving to buy a Christmas present for his mother, on lights for that very tree. With no guarantee it would make any difference to Mrs. Wentzell's Christmas spirit.

"Christmas tree, Christmas tree," Jonathan had said that day in school, when they were trying to figure out what to do next. "She definitely needs a Christmas tree."

The plan was to go to her house, hide out until it got dark, then do a quick decorating job on the fir tree.

"Lights," Jonathan had said. "Definitely lights. After the mess-up with the telephone, we got to do something she'll never forget."

Still, Jesse had stood a long time in the store, in front of the Christmas decorations, fingering the money in his pocket. Even though the set of lights was on sale. Even though Jonathan stood next to him and said, "But if it works, it'll be the best Christmas ever for your mother!"

"If. Big if."

He reluctantly pulled the money from his pocket.

And now they found themselves in their old spot, in the trees near Mrs. Wentzell's, peering through the branches at her house, Jonathan with the string of lights in his hands and Jesse with the extension cord in his. They had borrowed the cord from Jonathan's basement.

All her curtains were closed. "Now it's plenty dark," Jonathan whispered. "She'd never recognize us, even if the front door flies open and out she pops on the front step."

They rose up, a pair of Christmas gnomes, inching their way across her front yard. At the tree they stretched out the string of lights.

They looked up at the top branches. Neither of them could ever reach that high.

They looked at each other. There could be no argument about who was the heavier and had the broader back. Jonathan sank to the snow. Jesse put one foot on his back, then gingerly brought the other up from the ground to meet it. With a wobbling stretch, Jesse hooked the end of the string over the very top branch . . . before tumbling back to the ground!

He jumped up and grabbed the string of lights. Around and around the tree he went, until he ran out of lights. The bottom half of the tree was still bare.

"I knew we'd need another set," said Jonathan.

"Yeah, right. Forget it."

Jesse took one end of the extension cord and pushed the plug from the lights into it. He handed Jonathan the other end.

"Go for it," he said, pointing to the electric outlet on the side of the house, next to the front door. "I'll wait for you in the trees."

"Why me?"

But Jesse had already scrambled off.

From the hiding spot he could see Jonathan trying desperately to get the plug in the socket. The lights blinked once, then again, and finally lit up the tree!

The top half of it. Red and green and gold and blue, wonderful beacons of Christmas color.

"Whaddya think?" Jonathan said, out of breath, as he scampered into the hiding spot. "Think this will do it?"

Jonathan had an answer to his question soon enough. Mrs. Wentzell, in a great fur coat and slippers, opened the front door and stood there, stiff as a statue. In shock, maybe?

She let out a great grumble. "What now!"

Jesse and Jonathan stared at each other in disbelief.

"And what do you think the police will have to say about this?" she yelled, as if she knew someone was out there. "Tell me, what?" She stood rigid, like a glowering winter witch, scanning the front yard and surrounding trees. "I dare you to show your face!"

Their faces plunged instantly into the snow. And stayed there. Jesse's cheeks were stinging with the cold. And burning and freezing . . . until he could hardly stand another second of it.

He heard the door close.

He hauled up his head. He clawed the snow off his face and out of his eyes. Just in time to see Jonathan scraping and shaking his own snowman head.

"I'm outta here," Jonathan spit out with a spray of snow. He scurried backward, like a mole in reverse.

"Wait . . . "

"C'mon."

"What about the lights? The extension cord? The cops could trace them."

It stopped Jonathan dead in his tracks.

"You got to get the extension cord," he declared. *"I* plugged it in."

Jesse groaned at the thought of it. He gazed across the front yard and spied the outlet and the yellow cord coiling over the snow, like a cowardly snake.

He bit his teeth hard against each other. He drew in a chestful of air between them.

"Go for it!" Jonathan barked under his breath. "I'll get the lights."

Jesse sprang from the snow. He ran as hard as he could across the driveway, across the front yard, his eyes fixed all the time on the electrical outlet and its snake of a cord.

He was almost there when the front door opened. Jesse hit the snow!

Out scampered Ivan the Terrier. The front door closed again.

Jesse did not budge. He lay there as stiff as a lawn ornament. He heard the flutter of Ivan's short legs over the snow toward him. He felt the poke of Ivan's nose against his head.

Jesse opened one eye and looked up, straight into Ivan's underbelly. Ivan's hind leg started to rise!

Gross! Jesse flung himself to his feet.

He grabbed the extension cord from the snow and gave it an almighty yank! It snapped free from the outlet. Its recoil whizzed past Ivan's head.

The dog went berserk. It made for Jesse, yapping and yelping like crazy.

Jesse made for the tree. There was Jonathan, the string of lights free from the branches, except for the end of it hooked over the very top.

Jesse did not stop. He grabbed the lights from Jonathan with his other hand and kept on running. The top of the tree bent down behind him. The string of lights pulled tight and tighter — then snapped free!

Off the boys went like mad, through the snow, down the driveway, onto the main road, the extension cord and the string of lights trailing behind them. Ivan the Terrier in pursuit — scurrying as fast as his stumpy legs could carry him, his barking worse than a police siren.

Finally the dog ran out of steam. He stood and yelped as the boys raced away in the distance.

Jesse glanced over his shoulder. Ivan was trotting leisurely back up the driveway. His owner was calling. "Did you do your business? Did you do your business?"

All that evening the echo of Mrs. Wentzell's voice rang in Jesse's ears. That and his mother's angry words for his staying out after dark without anyone knowing where he and Jonathan had gone.

"More of that secret project, I suppose?"

Jesse would not tell exactly what they had been doing. He thought his explanation of buying a surprise present at the convenience store should be enough to satisfy her.

It wasn't. She even put Santa on her side.

She sat him on the kitchen table as Jesse was eating his bedtime snack. "In the House of Wooden Santas . . . " she began, anger still in her voice.

"That's not very nice. You're supposed to be mad at me, not him."

"In the House of Wooden Santas," she repeated. (A little too sweet, Jesse thought, but he figured it was best if he didn't say anything.) "There's a Santa who is not pleased with children who do not tell the *whole* story."

"But Santa knows the whole story," Jesse said. "He's part of it."

"Part of what?"

"That's a secret. See, Santa is not telling either."

"Not telling what?"

"Secret Santa doesn't like tricks." Jesse grinned broadly at his mother, then looked at the figure again. "Do you, *Secret Santa?"*

Jesse waited as his mother rolled her eyes.

"See," said Jesse, "he's not saying a word."

FIVE DAYS TO CHRISTMAS

Jesse answered the phone. He was still in his pajamas.

"I know your mother is there and you can't talk about you know who. Right?" It was Jonathan.

"Right," Jesse said sleepily.

"And us doing you know what, right?"

"Right."

"I just had to tell you that I woke up with this super fantastic plan to get you know who to do you know what. You won't believe it. Wait till I see you. Bye. And tell your mother you're asking me over to your place after school."

Jesse's mother gave him an odd look as he hung up the phone.

"It was only Jonathan."

"What are you fellows up to now?"

"Us?"

"Yes," his mother said, staring at him intently.

"Nothing." It was tough to come up with something better when his eyes were barely open. "He's coming over after school, that's all."

Jesse gave her the sweetest look he could muster.

He took off to get dressed for school. He was out the door with a kiss and ten minutes to spare.

Jonathan was waiting for him when he stepped off the bus. He was jumping up and down, trying to keep warm in the midst of the snow swirling across the parking lot.

He led Jesse to a corner of the school, out of the wind.

"Okay, ready for this?" Jonathan said.

"Yeah. C'mon. Hurry up."

"Do you think Mrs. Wentzell hangs a stocking at Christmas?"

"Of course not."

From his backpack he hauled out a large wool sock. "This is the biggest one I could find. It's Dad's. We fill it up with all kinds of stuff and we leave it on Mrs. Wentzell's doorstep." Jonathan stood tall and silent, as if he were waiting for applause.

Jesse screwed up his face. On her doorstep! After what happened? He must be crazy.

"It's clean," Jonathan said. "I smelled it."

"What kind of stuff?" Jesse said, just to make him think he was considering it.

"You know, *stuff.*"

"We haven't got any money left to buy *stuff.* Remember? We spent it on lights. Remember!"

"We'll use what we already got."

At recess Jonathan snatched away Jesse's apple just as he was about to bite into it. "Item number one," he said. Then from the dark reaches of his desk he dug out several snack boxes of raisins, leftovers from recesses long past. "Old people love these," he declared.

By the time they reached Jesse's house that afternoon the foot part of the stocking was nearly filled. Added to the food was an unsharpened pencil that glowed green in the dark; a reindeer ornament made with a clothespin, pipe cleaners, and a tiny red cotton ball; an eraser that smelled like grapes; and a bookmark in the shape of a Christmas monkey, with a gold-colored tassel for a tail. The last item had belonged to a girl in his math group and had cost Jesse three of his best markers.

At Jesse's house they were hit with a smell that instantly turned on another light in Jonathan's brain.

"Gingerbread," Jonathan said. "Good old-fashioned gingerbread. And old-fashioned people love it!"

"Even if they're not so good."

Jesse's mother had one batch of cookies in the oven and had rolled flat a second pile of dough.

She let them do the cutting. They washed their hands and went to work. They made stars and angels and snowmen, and out of sight of Jesse's mother they made a gingerbread woman with a smile that stretched from one of her dangling earrings to the other.

When they sneaked her into the oven to bake, Jesse declared, "This might warm her heart."

"Yes, sir," said Jonathan. "Yes, sir!"

After the gingerbread woman reappeared and was set out to cool, the boys whisked her away to Jesse's bedroom and packed her in a small box with some tissues. Down the sock she went.

"Now," said Jonathan, "what else you got?"

They scanned Jesse's room. Then turned to his junk drawer and treasure boxes.

The first find was an elf key chain. "Perfect," said Jonathan who had become the undisputed expert in what they could include and what they could not. He dug through it all, holding some of it up for a closer look. What he finally decided on was a pack of Old Maid cards, a sign for hanging on a doorknob that read: *Beware — adults enter at your own risk*, and a bunch of stickers from the dentist's office that had elephants on them with big, toothy grins.

And a Christmas tree ornament that was a Santa playing hockey.

"Can't have that," said Jesse.

"C'mon."

"No."

"C'mon."

"My dad sent it to me." He took it out of Jonathan's hand and put it back in the box. It was the first time he had mentioned his father in front of Jonathan.

"Will you see him at Christmas?"

"Doubt it."

Jesse gave Jonathan a look that said he didn't want to talk about it anymore.

By the time Jonathan's mother came by to pick him up, the stocking was two-thirds full. It made a bulge in Jonathan's backpack.

As he was leaving he whispered to Jesse, "I'll get more stuff at home. I'll stuff that sock till it can't hold another thing."

Their mothers were doing some whispering of their own.

" . . . nothing else either of us can do," Jesse's mother said as Reverend Agnew was going out the door.

The boys looked at each other. Jonathan winked.

A lopsided smile was the best Jesse could come up with.

His mother was in an even worse mood. And partway through their meal that evening she muttered, "I've been thinking about it all day. . . . I'm not sending that craft shop the new Santa. In fact, I'm not sending them any more Santas. There's no point in even making — "

"No way. You can't give up!" Jesse couldn't believe it.

His reaction startled his mother so much she dropped her fork.

"You just can't," Jesse declared. "I won't let you."

"But — "

"No buts." Jesse got up from the table. "Where is he?" There was desperation in his voice.

Jesse tramped off to the workroom. He returned with Santa and placed him in the middle of the table.

"See what I mean," his mother said. "Just look at him. I thought if I went kinda wild he might sell."

He sure wasn't like any of the others. But that was no reason to give up. "He's just different, that's all."

"Crazy, you mean."

"C'mon, start," Jesse said. "Come on."

There was the edge of a smile on his mother's face. "In the House of Wooden Santas there's . . . "

"Come on."

"I'm thinking. I'm thinking."

"There's . . . "

"There's a fellow who always keeps you on your toes. There's . . . there's . . . "

"I'm waiting."

"There's someone who's not afraid to jump off the deep end. There's a guy who's always full of surprises."

"That's it. He's our *Surprise Santa.*"

His mother's smile had grown to full size. She shook her head. "Never a dull moment with him around."

"Yep."

"Wonder what other surprises he might have?"

"You never know," said Jesse. "You just never know."

FOUR DAYS TO CHRISTMAS

Jesse was excited about his mother coming to his classroom that afternoon.

Mr. O'Donnell was even more excited. "What a treat, boys and girls. Imagine creating Santa Clauses all day long!"

When Jesse's mom finally walked through the door the children burst into cheers. All except Jesse, who was feeling a bit embarrassed by it all.

"Well," his mother said, "you sure have boosted my Christmas spirit."

Jesse liked it better when everyone turned quiet and his mother talked about her work — how she picked the wood and how she came up with the ideas. She laid out all her carving tools, then some brushes and pots of paint. She held up each tool and described how it was used. She passed around pictures of the first angels she ever made.

And finally the moment they had all been waiting for. From a box, under several layers of crumpled newspaper, she removed a Santa.

"From the House of Wooden Santas," his mother said, holding him up for everyone to see, "rides a world-famous traveler. He's pedaled over to see you today as a practice run, for Christmas Eve."

"Where's his reindeer?" a girl called out.

"You know the rules — no animals in school."

The children laughed and cheered again.

"I think we'll call this guy *Schoolhouse Santa.* In your honor. He's a bit of a student, you know. He loves making lists."

She set him down on a desk.

She brought out a square piece of pine wood. "And soon this will be another dear old Santa."

There was a final round of cheers.

"Isn't she magical, boys and girls?" Mr. O'Donnell said. "Isn't she magical?"

She looked at Jesse and gave him a sly wink.

When the bell rang for the end of school the children filed past the teacher's desk, each one of them patting Santa on the head.

Only Jesse and Jonathan were left.

"You did a terrific job," said Jonathan. "Can Jesse come over to my house?"

"He means," said Jesse when he saw that his mother wasn't quite ready for the question, "can I go over because we're working on that project."

"Oh, *that* project," she said.

She looked at them both, waiting for more. The boys shrugged. She looked at Mr. O'Donnell. He winked.

"I guess so," she said to Jesse.

DUNCAN
LUKE
ANNE
KEVIN
INA
ROBERT
NYLA
ERIN
MATTHEW
LISA
ROBERT
SUE
NICOLE
Adele
JESSE

The boys left her and Mr. O'Donnell by themselves. He winked at her, thought Jesse, he actually winked at her.

"The two of them like each other . . . a lot," said Jonathan.

"Not my mom, no way."

"You saw it. And that can only mean one thing."

"It's Christmas," said Jesse firmly, as if that should put an end to it.

At Jonathan's house they went straight to his bedroom and shut the door. From under the bed Jonathan pulled out what he now called the "O.W. Christmas Sock." It was packed so tightly that it bulged grossly out of shape. Jonathan had tied the top of the sock shut with bright red ribbon in a double knot.

There was no time to lose. They put the sock in a plastic bag and headed downstairs.

They ran nearly all the way to Mrs. Wentzell's.

They hung back in the trees again to size up the situation before making a move. Her car was in the driveway.

Jonathan held the bag out to Jesse.

"This one was your idea," said Jesse.

"Yeah, but you're the one she wants to kick out of the house, remember?"

"So."

Jesse looked at the bag. He slowly reached his hand inside and withdrew the O.W. Christmas Sock.

He took a deep breath. He stood up. With the sock clutched firmly in his hand, its red ribbon fluttering, he charged in the direction of the house, a Christmas knight on a mission of great courage.

He made a wide sweep around the car and headed stoutheartedly up the walkway. He cast steely eyes to the right and left.

When he reached the front step he quickly strung the red ribbon through the handle of the door and tied it in a big bow.

"Hurry up," Jonathan hissed in his direction.

Jesse rang the doorbell and ran for the trees.

"See," he said to Jonathan. "Nothing to it. Didn't bother me one bit."

The two of them peered out from between the trees to see Mrs. Wentzell open her door and catch her first sight of the O.W. Christmas Sock. They loved the way she carefully untied the ribbon and held the lumpy load of good cheer in her hands. She looked all around, then retreated inside, just in time to prevent the escape of Ivan the Terrier.

Jesse wondered if she would yell out something, something loud and especially mean. She never did.

"The spirit of Christmas just came ringing," Jesse proclaimed as they strolled back down the road. "And Mrs. Wentzell opened the door to welcome it in!"

"We got to her this time!" Jonathan yelled. "Yes, sir! Old crabby will never be the same."

The boys headed home, feeling for all the world like a pair of Santa Clauses.

THREE DAYS TO CHRISTMAS

Inside the bathroom "Rudolph the Red-Nosed Reindeer" rang out. Jesse let his Christmas spirit run wild.

"Last day of school before the holidays," he announced when he came into the kitchen.

"Gee, I never would have guessed," his mother said.

"And something amazing is going to happen. I can feel it."

"What's that?"

"Can't say." Jesse grinned. "We'll just have to wait and see, won't we?"

At school he found Jonathan as wild as himself. During the Christmas party that afternoon the two of them went dancing and prancing like goofy reindeer.

A crazy excitement was running through the class. How they all wished for Christmas Day! They told Jesse they wished they could have a Santa-making mother just like his. "Then it would be Christmas every day of the year!"

Mr. O'Donnell joined in. "Yes, what a lucky fellow you are! What a special mom!"

Jesse gave Mr. O'Donnell a goofy reindeer face, as if it were all part of his Christmas craziness.

"Going anywhere for Christmas, sir?" Jesse called to him when school was finally over and he was heading out the door.

"Not this year."

Too bad, Jesse said to himself.

"See you in church, Jesse. If not before."

Jesse forced a smile.

When he arrived home from school that day, his Christmas spirit was still flying high. He burst into the house singing at the top of his lungs.

"Then one foggy Christmas Eve, Santa came to say . . . "

He kept it up while he got rid of his winter clothes — and while he scurried through the house in his sock feet looking for his mother.

He found her in the living room, sitting on the sofa in front of a fire. Behind her stood a bare Christmas tree.

He fell into her arms on one final note of his song. He drew back. She hadn't said a word.

"Mom, what's the matter?"

"I cut a Christmas tree. Do you like it? We'll have to decorate it soon."

"What happened?"

"It's okay. I took out the box of decorations. Why don't you try the lights first to see if they all work before we put them on."

Jesse didn't budge. He stared at his mother. "You got to tell me."

Finally she said, "I've been talking to Mrs. Wentzell."

All that day Jesse had imagined his mother saying those words, but it was never in the way she said them now.

"We're still behind on the rent. And someone else wants to rent the house. We have to be out of here in a week. It's definite."

Jesse was stunned. And suddenly miserable through and through.

"It's not fair!" he burst out.

All that work, for nothing!

All that time believing, when it was a useless thing to ever do!

His mother hugged him long and hard. Harder than she ever had before.

The doorbell rang. Jesse's mother went to answer it.

Through his misery Jesse could hear the voice of Reverend Agnew. "I told Jonathan. He had to come over right away."

They joined the black cloud in the living room. Jesse let loose a loud, sneering grumble. "There's no one more mean and heartless than Mrs. Wentzell!"

"She's a witch if there ever was one!" Jonathan burst out.

The boys sat on the floor in front of the fire, staring at it. The mothers watched them in silence.

Finally Reverend Agnew piped up, "I refuse to let that woman spoil Christmas."

"I agree," Jesse's mom added, but said nothing more.

"Now then," said Reverend Agnew. "How about I mix some eggnog? Someone put on some Christmas music. Someone open up that box of decorations for the tree."

The boys took their dead-slow time.

"Christmas slugs," Jonathan's mother said and poked them in the ribs to get them moving.

After a while it turned dark outside, the lights on the tree grew brighter, and a jazzy version of "Winter Wonderland" filled the room.

"Maybe it's time for a Santa," Jesse's mother said. "I think we're all in pretty desperate need of one."

"Forget it," said Jesse.

Jonathan shook his head. "No way."

"He let us down. We did our part. . . . "

The two mothers looked at each other. "What exactly *did* you do?"

The room fell silent, except for the music.

"It's a pretty big secret, I take it," said Reverend Agnew.

Not a word.

"Maybe Santa is still working on it," said Jesse's mother.

"I'd give him till Christmas Eve, wouldn't you?" added Reverend Agnew.

The boys grunted. They looked at their mothers with stronger doubts than ever.

Jesse's mother turned down the music and left the room. She returned with a Santa in her hands. She set him down near the boys, in front of the fire.

The boys would not look up at him.

"In the House of Wooden Santas we hope everything will turn out for the best."

"We hope and pray for it," said Reverend Agnew. "Saint Nicholas surely knows the power of prayer. He depends on more than his reindeer to get him around the world on Christmas Eve."

Jesse looked at Jonathan and then at the two mothers. "Yeah, right."

"Tell us another one," Jonathan grunted.

His mother jumped in. "He'll keep us in his prayers, especially now, when we need it most."

"Prayer Santa he is," said Jesse's mom.

The boys showed no sign they were even listening until Reverend Agnew began to pray for help through the tough times ahead. "Like lost sheep we are, O God. Help us to find the path to a safe and happy home."

Jesse and Jonathan muttered a stiff "Amen."

"Santa heard that, I bet," said Jesse's mom.

"And I'm sure God did," Jonathan's mother declared.

TWO DAYS TO CHRISTMAS

When Jesse awoke he had the crazy sensation he was still in school, that he wasn't on holidays, that it wasn't the day before Christmas Eve.

He was sure he heard a school voice, a very familiar one.

Only one person he knew sounded like that. But the voice was coming from the kitchen.

His mother was talking to Mr. O'Donnell in the kitchen, in their own house, on a Saturday morning!

Jesse bolted upright in bed. He rubbed his hands into his face and ears. The voice did not go away. In fact it seemed to grow louder and more pleased with itself.

Jesse crept to his door to hear what they were saying. It was nothing important. He sat back on the bed with relief.

"Mr. O'Donnell came by to see how we're doing," Jesse's mother said when Jesse showed up in the kitchen. "I invited him in for coffee. He brought some doughnuts . . . and a few other things. For Christmas."

Presents, thought Jesse. Oh, yeah. He wondered what besides coffee Mr. O'Donnell had on his mind.

"We're doing just fine, aren't we, love?" she said to Jesse.

"You've sold a few Santa Clauses, I bet," Mr. O'Donnell said, full of good cheer.

She hesitated. "One."

"I see." His surprise mixed with his disappointment. "And the shopping days are running ou . . . "

He looked sorry to have said it.

"After Christmas," he was quick to add. "You'll have better luck after Christmas. Angels sell all year long, I'd say."

"We won't be around to find out," Jesse declared.

Over Mr. O'Donnell's face came a severe frown. It seemed Jesse's mother hadn't told him a thing about Mrs. Wentzell.

Jesse blurted out the whole story — the great secret his mother had *not* shared with Mr. O'Donnell, even though the two of them might *never* see each other again.

To top off the whole story, Jesse announced, "And you won't be my teacher anymore, either."

His mother gave Jesse a very hard look.

She was about to say something to him when Mr. O'Donnell let out a sorry cry, "Not true."

"I would have told you. . . . "

"And absolutely nothing is going to change Mrs. Wentzell's mind," Jesse said. "I know that for a fact. She's a Christmas witch."

"She is that," said his mother.

"And," said Mr. O'Donnell, "she's my aunt."

Jesse winced.

So did his mother. "Not true," she said, her voice trailing away.

Mr. O'Donnell nodded. "It's a small place."

That didn't do much to help Jesse or his mother out of their embarrassment.

"She's a tough bird," Mr. O'Donnell said. "Especially since her husband died. That's why she's having so much fuss with the church. Uncle Marvin was a church warden for so long he thought he owned the place. I guess God is straightening him out on that one."

Mr. O'Donnell chuckled and that gave Jesse the courage to speak again. "Isn't there anyone who can make her change her mind?"

"When she sets that mind of hers to something . . . it's more than I can do to pry it loose."

His mother left the room. Jesse was not surprised when she returned with a new figure in her hands.

"Last Chance Santa," said Jesse, with a sneer.

She frowned.

"What do you mean, 'last chance'?" asked Mr. O'Donnell.

"He means last chance for him to be a good boy," his mother said firmly. "Or he might not get anything for Christmas."

Jesse didn't much care. "I mean last chance for Santa to prove he's for real," Jesse said decisively.

"Santa doesn't have to prove anything," Mr. O'Donnell piped up with a force that caused Jesse to promptly sit upright. "I, for one, believe. And I pity those who don't. Because they miss out on all the fun."

He tapped Jesse on the head with his finger.

"It's up to you," he said.

Jesse's mother was having a hard time coming up with the right words. "In the House of Wooden Santas . . . I guess this is the last chance for Jesse to make up his mind."

Jesse slipped out of the kitchen and sat on the sofa in the living room. He needed to be by himself, away from adults who try to sound like they know it all.

He looked around the room. The tree they decorated the night before had filled the house with a fresh evergreen smell. He thought back to the day his mother had put up the first Christmas decorations. He looked to the spot where the television used to be. He had almost forgotten about it.

His eyes turned to the mantel. He remembered the first Santa his mother had put there. And all the others that had appeared each day since. He missed them. He wished they all could be in this room at the same time. Maybe they'd help him make up his mind once and for all if there was a Santa Claus.

When he told his mother his wish she put down her coffee cup and thought about it for a long time before speaking. "Probably I should put the craft shop out of its misery and bring them back." She smiled. "And it would be great to see them all together."

"Except for one," Jesse reminded her.

"I'd love to go with you," said Mr. O'Donnell. "We could go in *my* car. Lots of room for Santas."

Jesse's mother thought it was a great idea. Jesse didn't say anything.

"Know what?" Mr. O'Donnell said to him. "On the way back we could stop by my place. I think I might be able to come up with that Santa you'd be missing."

Jesse shrugged.

"Hey, I paid good money for that guy," Mr. O'Donnell said, smiling. "Maybe I could be persuaded to let you borrow him . . . *if* you both agree to come to my place for Christmas dinner."

Jesse could feel their eyes on him, waiting for his answer.

"Sure, Mr. O'Donnell," he said. "Might as well. Since it looks like we'll never see you again."

ONE DAY TO CHRISTMAS

It was a wonderful sight, this trail of wooden Santas.

The line started on the mantel, descended down a stairway of boxes to two tables joined together, and came to an end in the spot where the television had been. Their way was lit by tiny lights woven through pine boughs. A lively crew they were, all bound for Christmas Day.

Jesse, still in his pajamas, sat with his mother on the sofa and followed the line from beginning to end, stopping at each one to remember what had happened on the day that particular Santa had appeared.

And the final fellow, which his mother had completed that morning, stood proudly at the end of the line.

Jesse mouthed the words of his mother, "In the House of Wooden Santas . . . " then sat back, as she continued. He was thinking of the long hours of her work lined up before him.

" . . . we have found a good bit of happiness, a few parts sadness, and lots of fun times together. *Santa of the Years Yet to Come* says that whatever comes our way, we got each other, you and me."

"But, Mom."

"But Mom what?"

"What about Mr. O'Donnell?"

"And what about Mr. O'Donnell?"

"Aren't you in love with him?"

"Jesse!" She drew back. "What a question."

But she wasn't answering it. Jesse began to squirm.

"No, I am not," she said after so much silence that Jesse thought it was never going to end.

She could have done better than that!

"Mr. O'Donnell . . . " she started, then stopped.

Jesse waited. What in the world was taking her so long?

"Mr. O'Donnell is a very nice man. But . . . I don't think you have anything to worry about."

"We're fine, just like we are," Jesse said.

"I think so." She added, "Even if we have to move?"

Jesse had been trying to put that part out of his mind. He just wanted to have a regular Christmas and not think about the rotten things to come afterward. He ignored his mother's question.

But he couldn't ignore Jonathan's.

Jonathan had phoned him, desperate to have one last try at getting Mrs. Wentzell to change her mind. "It's our only chance. Tomorrow is Christmas Day."

"And what would we do this time?" Jesse asked with a groan. "Cook a turkey and drop it on her doorstep?"

Jonathan was dead serious. "I think we should march straight up to her door and say what a rotten thing it is she's doing. And if she doesn't change her mind, we'll tell her off."

"Really?" said Jesse, who couldn't quite believe the eagerness in Jonathan's voice.

"I'm not chicken."

"Just crazy," said Jesse. "She'll call the police on us. She won't just stand there. She'll flatten us."

"And then we sue her! Then she'll have to change her mind."

Jonathan's idea was running wild. But still he wouldn't take no for an answer.

"What have we got to lose?" said Jonathan.

Not much, Jesse had to admit. The time for Mrs. Wentzell to change her mind had all but run out. It was now or never. And Jonathan certainly didn't sound like he was willing to stand by and let *never* come without a final fight.

So that afternoon Jesse found himself walking with Jonathan up the road to Mrs. Wentzell's, the one they had walked so many times before, and every time for nothing.

Jesse tried to stay cool and forget the butterflies that were swarming around his insides. Jonathan was trying even harder. He sang some mad, mixed-up version of "The Twelve Days of Christmas" and fired snowballs at nothing in particular.

They came to the trees where they had hidden themselves before and walked right past them. They came to Mrs. Wentzell's car parked in the driveway and walked right past it.

They stepped on the carefully shoveled path that led right to Mrs. Wentzell's front door, and Jesse said, "I'm not so sure about this," and hoped he didn't sound like a coward.

"Too late now," Jonathan shot back. He continued his march, not missing a step. He pulled off his mitt and stuck his finger on the doorbell just as Jesse caught up with him.

The door swung open immediately.

There stood Mrs. Wentzell, Ivan the Terrier in her arms. The dog started to yelp.

"I saw you coming," Mrs. Wentzell announced.

Jonathan looked her in the eye. And fell dead silent. He couldn't get a word out.

Ivan yelped and yelped, as if he were the one to do all the talking.

Mrs. Wentzell finally shut his mouth with her hand. "Well?" she said to the boys.

"Mrs. Wentzell," stammered Jesse, "Jonathan has something to tell you."

She looked at Jonathan, but Jonathan's tongue was in knots and he was making less sense than the dog.

"Mrs. Wentzell," Jesse began again, "Won't you change your mind? We *can't* go."

"That nephew of mine put you up to this, didn't he?"

Jesse realized the nephew she was talking about was Mr. O'Donnell.

"When he told me he was in church last Sunday I nearly choked. Just because he likes your mother, that's no reason he should be telling me what to do."

Ivan the Terrier's mouth broke free from her hand and he let out a vicious bark, as if to emphasize her point.

Jesse suddenly felt his mother's fighting streak stirring deep inside him. It rose from his stomach, up his swelling chest, and spewed out his mouth in a torrent of fiery words.

"Not fair! You're being a Christmas witch! You don't care about anything or anybody, only yourself. You got a letter from Santa and Christmas music and your tree all lit up. . . . "

"And my dad's stocking full of stuff!" Jonathan stammered.

Mrs. Wentzell's eyebrows stiffened severely.

The cat had been let out of the bag. Ivan yelped louder than ever.

"So," droned Mrs. Wentzell, "I suspected as much."

It was clearly a standoff.

Mrs. Wentzell let her mutt bark all he wanted, as if she were threatening to let him loose to chew off their legs. The boys stood their ground in steaming silence.

Finally Mrs. Wentzell retreated. She stepped backward and took hold of the door handle.

"Don't you know the meaning of Christmas, Mrs. Wentzell?" exclaimed Jesse in one last burst of frustration.

She looked at both the boys, their ruddy expressions stiff and sour, but she did not answer. She closed the door in their faces.

The boys stood there for a second. Then they, too, retreated, winding their way back up the road.

The rest of the afternoon Jesse spent thinking about what they had done. It didn't put him in any mood for Christmas.

That evening he sat on the sofa, his shepherd's staff across his lap, waiting for his mother to finish dressing so they could leave for the Christmas Eve service at church. He looked along the row of Santas.

How could he believe when they never came through for him? He and Jonathan had done all they could. Santa was no more than a wooden statue who sat all Christmas on a shelf, pretending to be real.

He heard his mother heading for the door. His lip curled into a sneer. "Fake," he muttered as he left the room. He didn't bother to look back.

They were met at the church door by Reverend Agnew and a flurry of guitar and piano music coming from the front of the church. The place was filling up, with more people arriving all the time. Reverend Agnew hugged his mom and directed Jesse to the room at the back of the church.

There he found Jonathan dressed in his shepherd outfit, staff in hand. Jesse dressed in a hurry, and the two stood together, two sorrowful shepherds, hardly saying a word to each other.

"Cheer up," Reverend Agnew told them. "You look like two lost sheep." Neither of them smiled.

Later, when they stood before the congregation, one on either side of the stable, they still looked a pitiful pair.

Jesse's mother caught his eye. She kept pointing to her mouth and flashing a smile.

No way, Jesse said to himself.

Then he caught sight of Mrs. Wentzell! There, behind his mother. She had come in through the back door and was slowly walking up the aisle to take a seat.

"Look," Jesse muttered under his breath to Jonathan.

Their stares were interrupted by Reverend Agnew. "Tonight," she said in a voice that filled the church, "we celebrate the coming of the Child. A child for all the world — innocent and loving, playful and caring, forever hopeful."

With each word the boys straightened up a little more.

"This Child is the child in all of us," Reverend Agnew said over the squawks of several babies in the congregation.

She nodded to the boys. They opened the doors to the stable.

They revealed an infant lying in a manger. And around the infant a semicircle of other figures. Two of them were shepherds.

"Dad's shepherds?" whispered Jonathan.

"Yeah," said Jesse.

The boys looked out into the rows of faces and saw Jonathan's dad. He was smiling their way.

All the people sang "Away in a Manager," every word strong and clear.

The boys walked back down the aisle on the last verse, past Jonathan's dad, who had a wink for them, and Jesse's mom, who was wiping her eyes, and Mr. O'Donnell, who was grinning proudly, and Mrs. Wentzell, who was trying to sing but couldn't seem to get all the words out, especially when the boys blurted, "Merry Christmas," to her as they went by.

Later, when the church service was over, the boys gathered with Jonathan's parents for a closer look at the nativity scene.

"We look cool in there," said Jesse.

"And you wanted Dad to make a Christmas moose," Jonathan reminded him.

Mr. Agnew chuckled.

"A marvelous pair," Jesse's mother said, joining them, Mr. O'Donnell right behind her.

They all stood together in the glow of the light shining down on the manger.

Only Jesse saw Mrs. Wentzell approach. Only he had seen her come back in the church after everyone else had gone.

"Could I have a look?" she asked quietly.

The others turned and discovered her standing there. It was a surprise they could not hide. They moved aside to make room for her.

"Of course," said Reverend Agnew.

She drew closer and stared at the figures for a long time.

"My husband always loved the nativity scene," she said. "Christmas was always his favorite time of the year." She picked up one of the shepherds. "Christmas is not the same when it's just yourself."

She replaced the shepherd and started to leave.

She turned back, hesitantly. "I didn't want to come to church this evening, but I had to. It's Christmas Eve. Marvin would never have forgiven me."

She looked at the boys. "I hardly knew what to do. I guess I was like the sheep looking for a shepherd."

She reached out and touched Jesse's staff.

"And when you two opened the stable doors it was like I was seeing inside for the first time. A child again."

For several moments everyone was quiet. There was something else on her mind and she was having a hard time getting it out. "This church needs all you young people," she said finally.

"And old people, too," Jesse said.

"Yeah," said Jonathan. "Right, Mom?"

Reverend Agnew reached out and squeezed her hand.

Mrs. Wentzell said, "I'll be going now. I need to phone my daughter."

She smiled awkwardly and walked away, heading to the back door again.

"Mrs. Wentzell," Jesse's mother called. "I would like you to come and visit us. Tonight?" She looked at the others. "All of you come. It's Christmas Eve."

Mrs. Wentzell hesitated. She looked at Jesse and Jonathan. "Two shepherds and a Christmas witch?"

It sent both of them stammering. Then Jesse said, "But now you got the Christmas spirit."

"And a letter and sock to prove it," said Mrs. Wentzell.

There was a trickle of uncomfortable laughter. The parents looked at each other, perplexed, but joined in.

They carried it along to Jesse's house that night. When Mrs. Wentzell arrived she encountered the winding trail of Santas.

"And tonight of course," said Jesse's mother, handing her a cup of tea, "the fellow himself shows up. The real one."

"He'll be amazed," said Mrs. Wentzell.

She leaned forward for a longer, admiring look at each Santa.

"Mr. O'Donnell owns one," said Jesse, and pointed him out.

His mother whispered something in Jesse's ear.

Jesse thought hard for a moment, then removed *Hockey Santa* from the lineup. "Jonathan owns another." He handed the Santa to him. "It's from Mom and me. Thanks for the rink."

"Wicked," said Jonathan, clutching the fellow.

"I have an idea," said Mrs. Wentzell, being very serious, but with excitement in her voice they had not heard before.

They all listened intently.

"May I choose a couple as payment for the rent you missed?"

"Really?" said Jesse's mom. It caught her completely by surprise.

"My granddaughter would love one. And my daughter."

"It would have to be more. . . . "

"And a few more for the weeks coming up. And maybe some time after that. There are other people I could be giving presents to this Christmas. They'd be thrilled."

"Thrilled enough to come and buy another one?" asked Mr. O'Donnell with a certain mischievous note in his voice.

"Who knows?" said Mrs. Wentzell. "Though your side of the family is pretty tight."

She took great pleasure in seeing Mr. O'Donnell stumble about for words.

"Once the charm of Santa Claus takes hold," she said, "you never know what can happen."

Mrs. Wentzell departed that night with a box packed with enough Santas to keep Jesse and his mother in the house for a couple of months.

Mr. O'Donnell left with his Santa and with a promise to Jesse and his mom that for their Christmas dinner the next day there would be a plump turkey and flaming pudding *and* chestnuts roasting over his open fire.

Jonathan and his parents were the last to go.

"Now I have competition," said Jesse's mom to Mr. Agnew.

"Not for long. Just until the day I can walk with a hammer in one hand and a saw in the other."

Reverend Agnew thanked Jesse's mother again for giving him the idea to start carving. "I don't know what he would have done."

"Driven us nuts," said Jonathan.

His dad made a playful swipe at his rear end with his walking stick. "Is that so?"

"Yep."

He chased Jonathan out the door.

Reverend Agnew was not long after them. "For heaven's sake, be careful! If one of you falls and ends up in a cast, so help me, I'll send the both of you out to pasture!"

Jesse and his mom stood laughing in the doorway.

"Merry Christmas!"

"Merry Christmas!" the others called back from inside their car as they drove away.

It was getting late. And time for Jesse to be heading to bed.

Jesse hung his stocking by the fireplace and sat with his mom on the sofa for a last few minutes, his feet wedged between the cushions, hot chocolate in his hand. The trail of Santas had several gaps now, and perhaps, before Christmas was over, there would be many more.

"You got to believe," said Jesse, between slurps of hot chocolate.

His mother looked at him, but didn't say a word. She put her arm around his shoulder.

"If you didn't believe in something because you couldn't see it, then your life would be very boring," he said. "Right?"

He looked into his mother's eyes until she nodded.

"A carving shows us the good stuff, like friends and stuff, and love, right?" This time he couldn't wait for her to answer. "And if we didn't believe in that, we'd never have it."

She squeezed him so hard there seemed to be Santas dancing before his eyes.

And off he went toward his room, full of love and full of excitement about what Christmas Day would bring.

Before he reached there the telephone rang.

His mother started toward it, but then she said, "You answer it, okay?"

It was his father.

"Guess what?" Jesse said. "So far this has been my best Christmas ever."

There was a long pause.

"You gotta believe it," he said. "We're doing great."

Jesse listened to his father telling him there was a present in the mail for him and he was sorry it was going to be a little late getting there.

"That's okay," said Jesse, "Santa Claus will be on time." He told his dad he loved him and then he said good-bye.

His mother put her arms around Jesse, and after a second try, managed to pick him up. She dropped him into bed.

"Good-night, love."

"Thanks for all your hard work, Mom." He gave her a kiss. "But, Mom, I don't have a Christmas present for you."

"You're my Christmas present," she said, and gave him a slobbery kiss.

He smiled and wiped his cheek.

He curled under the covers and shut his eyes tightly, and immediately, without a murmur, started to count sheep.